The Price of Friendship

Dimensional Destinies Book One

By Philip Carroll

Published by Philip Carroll, Author

Modesto, California

February 2019

Edited by Jen Hendricks

ISBN (ebook) 978-0-9990496-4-8

ISBN (paperback) 978-0-9990496-5-5

1

Dedication

Since this book began as a short story based on a prompt on the Great Hites Podcast, I would like to dedicate it to Jeff and all my friends who started me in the podcasting world. That would include Lawrence Simon at the 100 Word Weekly Challenge Podcast, Zach Ricks and all my friends from Flying Island Press, Podiobooks.com (which no longer exists), Nathan Lowell, the late P.G. Holyfield, Chooch and Viv Schubert of the City of Heroes Podcast, and all others who have inspired me to write, record, and publish.

1 - A Pound of Flesh

"Mr. Baker. You appear to be semi-conscious. Can you repeat what I have just said?" Chad looked up from his book to see the teacher glaring directly at him. A permanent red blush gave her face the appearance of a wrinkled red apple with an unkempt mass of steel wool perched atop it.

She added in a mutter, but loud enough for the entire class to hear, "It is doubtful that any of you could make the logical correlation it would take to explain this on your own."

A sinking feeling in his stomach reminded him he understood the correlation all too well.

"Mrs. Walker?" He stammered and scratched at his short blond hair.

The teacher appeared to inflate, rising up in her chair like a tired helium balloon. She narrowed her bulbous frog-eyes and pressed her colorless lips into a thin, flat line. Her nostrils whistled a long, slow hiss as she inhaled for what he knew would be an explosive tirade. You couldn't show weakness in Mrs. Walker's classroom without feeling the sarcastic bite of her condescending wit. All the students knew hesitation and indecision were weakness in the elderly teacher's mind. Chad quickly launched into a reply before she could get started, repeating as best as he could remember. "You said the term, 'A pound of flesh', used in Shakespeare's play *The Merchant of Venice* has become synonymous with an onerous, undesirable debt that must be repaid."

The surprise evident on her face was a brilliant contrast to the dread on his own. He understood completely what it meant to have an onerous debt. In fact, the payment of his own pound of flesh might be made in just a few hours.

"Since you are so very clever," the teacher said, placing sarcastic emphasis on the last word, "maybe you could give us an example of this kind of debt in a way your fellow, less astute classmates might understand?" She flashed what Chad felt was her most evil and conniving grin.

The old woman hated children. Chad figured she was still a teacher only so she could exact revenge for an offense against her earlier in her career. It must have been pretty bad to have made her bitterness endure this long.

Mr. Walker had been a well-liked, unassuming, and kindly florist. Within months of their sudden and unexpected marriage, he died mysteriously in his sleep. No cause of death was ever determined and no charges were filed. Rumors said she was so mean she even killed her husband with a single, lethal, cynical comment. Forty years later, his widow remained a teacher, and alone.

Chad stared at Mrs. Walker as the blood drained from his face. He opened and closed his mouth several times, feeling like a fish, glassy eyed and pale. He was hesitating again. The only thing that would come to his mind as an example would reveal his own complex and embarrassing situation.

The old woman saw the hesitation and added with an evil smirk, "And why don't you come stand in front of the class, so everyone can hear you clearly?"

Chad blushed so deeply the freckles across his nose and cheekbones completely disappeared. He dragged his feet as he walked to the front of the classroom. His mind raced for an example from a movie or a TV show the students could relate to. Then it came to him. These were eighth-graders. They all understood peer pressure.

"An onerous debt is like," he began and stopped suddenly.

Everyone in the class was staring at him. Some were making faces, or mouthing threats. Though he was average sized for his age, neither skinny nor muscular, he suddenly felt small in his baggy t-shirt. He felt like he was back in sixth grade, when he'd grown so much his ankles were sticking out below too-short blue jeans.

He thought to himself, "They're laughing at me. And why not? What makes me qualified to tell the class anything? There are tons of kids here smarter than me."

"Umm," he paused as his mind went blank again. He began to panic, sweating as his vision went red around the edges. He just wanted to sit back down and disappear.

To his horror, words poured out of his mouth, "It's like when you borrow something from someone you know you shouldn't borrow anything from, because if it gets lost or broken, they'll kill you and then when you realize it's broken and they're going to beat you up, you..."

He was rambling and saying everything he had wanted to keep to himself. He stopped and looked around at his fellow students. They stared back, blankly, as stunned by his rapid delivery as he was. He glanced at the teacher who was nodding her head in agreement. He took that as affirmation and made his way back to his seat, doing his best to disappear until class ended and he could make his escape.

Outside, a series of large oak trees formed a line from one wing of the junior high school, behind the third base bleachers of the baseball field all the way to the basketball courts, delineating the far end of the outdoor grassy area where the students ate their lunch. Each tree had benches forming an octagon around the base of its trunk, so the students could eat their lunches under the protection of the spreading branches.

Chad sat in his usual spot, under the tree farthest from the basketball courts. His normal group of friends arrived one by one to eat their lunches. He didn't eat. He just looked despondently at his sandwich. Amy came last and headed to the empty place next to Chad. He was so absorbed by dread he didn't even notice her sitting down. Amy stared at him for a long moment. When he failed to acknowledge her, she turned and started a conversation with one of her girlfriends.

A tall, dark-haired boy, Derrick, walked up to them. "I hear Walker was picking on you today, Chad."

His heart froze. The boy kicked Chad's foot when he didn't respond, and asked good naturedly, "What did you do to make her so mad at you?"

Chad looked up at Derrick who was smiling down at him. "I don't know. She's just mean, and she needed someone to pick on. It just happened last period. How'd you hear about it?"

The taller boy didn't reply. He just barked a short, forced laugh.

Amy turned to them and said, "I don't think she intends to be mean. I know she comes across that way, but I think she's really just sad. Carol Ann said she sees Mrs. Walker driving past their house every Saturday morning, early, like before seven. Carol Ann said she goes to the cemetery and visits her husband's grave."

"Probably checking to make sure he's still dead," another boy, Tony, said too loudly, and laughed even louder. It wasn't funny, but all the boys joined in out of loyalty to their gender.

Amy was about to continue her defense of Mrs. Walker when the bell rang, ending their lunch. As they all got to their feet, she asked, "Well, I'll see you after choir, Chad?"

"Sure." He watched her turn and walk off. He thought about how pretty she was, her wavy brown hair falling just past her shoulders. She was a bit shorter than most girls, but not fat, and she always dressed nicely. He admired her choice of sweater and blue jeans and thought about the last school dance—the night had ended with a slow song. He got to stand close to her, feeling her body against his, breathing in the scent of her hair as it tickled his nose.

Derrick startled him from his revelry.

"You have my game, right?" he demanded, stepping in close. Chad tried to step back, intimidated by the larger boy's proximity and the menacing tone in his voice. Unfortunately, the bench was right behind Chad and it buckled his knees. He dropped suddenly to sit on the hard wooden surface. Chad looked around for help. The rest of his friends were halfway back to the school and clearly out of hearing distance.

"Yeah, Derrick, I have the game. It's in my locker, but—"

Derrick interrupted him, his already threatening eyes turning even colder. "But what?" he snarled, bending over and grabbing the front of Chad's shirt.

"I don't know," Chad started lamely. "I never played it. When I got home, I took it out of my backpack and it wouldn't work. It wouldn't even come on."

"You broke my game?" Derrick let go of Chad's shirt and pushed him back at the same time. "My Dad's going to kill me." He turned from side to side, opening and closing his hands like he was trying to squeeze something out of the air. His face turned from grey to pink to red, and was approaching purple, when Derrick stopped and pointed his finger at Chad. The boy's whole body shook, and though his eyes were as black as his hair, they burned with fire. He growled at Chad, "You're going to pay! You're going to pay for that game. I'm telling you."

"I can't pay for it. I don't have any money, and my mom is still out of work. I don't even have a bike! What can I give you?" He was getting frantic and it reflected clearly in his voice.

Derrick stopped, dead still, his head tilted to the side and up. He looked as if he was listening to a far-off voice, its message coming to him in pieces on the wind. A smile spread slowly across his face, and he looked like a cat that had just trapped a mouse.

"I know what you can give me. Your girlfriend. Bring her to the first base dugout after school." Without waiting for a reply, Derrick turned and strode toward the building.

2 - Setting the Trap

Chad slipped into his science class a few minutes after the bell rang. The class hadn't settled down enough for anyone to notice his late arrival. He sat and tried to think of what he would say to Amy.

She wasn't really a girlfriend, not in the sense they were going out. They didn't hold hands at lunch or make out in the halls between classes, like a lot of the kids did. But to fit in as an eighth-grade boy, you had to have a girlfriend, so when the other boys asked who it was, he would tell them it was Amy. He was sure his saying so must have gotten back to her. She still sat with him at lunch time, though. And if he waited for her to get out of her choir class after school, she would walk home with him. So, she must not have minded he was saying so.

Not wanting to get caught with a cellphone out in class, Chad opened a notebook and began to write out a note explaining his predicament. Amy was in his civics class next period and that would give him the opportunity to slip her the note before she went to choir practice. In it he explained everything that happened, and what he thought would come next, but as he proofread it, it sounded unbelievably lame. What kind of jerk would think he could give a girl away? Even if he gave her the note, she would never show up. He folded it over and over, then he shoved it in his back pocket, intending to burn it or flush it down the toilet. On a new piece of paper, he wrote, *Amy, meet me at the lunch tree after choir. I need to talk to you. Chad.* He folded this one in half three times, wrote her name on the front, and put it in the front pocket of his backpack.

He'd spent so much time composing his letters that class was ending. Hurrying out the door, he quickly walked to his last class of the day.

In civics he and Amy sat on opposite sides of the classroom, but as soon as he entered he walked straight over to where she sat. He gave her a weak smile and dropped the note on her desk, trying to look as nonchalant as possible. He didn't want to draw any attention to Amy or himself. Quickly he turned so she couldn't grill him with questions until after class.

He got to his seat as the teacher stood and began to address the class. He snuck a glance at Amy who had just finished reading the note. As he watched, she carefully folded it and put it in her backpack. She looked across the room at him and frowned. Then she shrugged her shoulders and nodded.

While the teacher was droning about amendments to the Constitution, Chad felt dreadful. He stole another quick look at Amy leaning over her book. From where he sat, he could only see the back of her head, her cheekbone, and her small roundish nose. He felt like a traitor delivering a faithful friend to suffer the penalties of his personal crimes. But, what crime had he committed?

Chad's mind kept turning to questions about Derrick. He really didn't know much about the other boy. He figured Derrick was new to the school, though they had never really talked about it. He just appeared one day, at their lunch tree, talking like they were old friends and he had been hanging out there since spring break. He wasn't in any of Chad's other classes and they seldom saw each other in the hallway.

"Chad! Hello, Chad?" Chad looked up as the teacher called out his name. He must have missed her first address, because most of the class had turned to look at him. "Yes, Ms. Van Doorn? I'm sorry, what did you say?" he replied, blushing.

"Well, I never knew my lectures were so absorbing. Deep in thought about human rights?" she asked lightly.

"Oh, yes, ma'am. Kind of." This was not his day for staying out of the spotlight.

"Chad, you're wanted in the principal's office." As she watched his face turn from bright red to milk pale, she tried to lighten the situation by saying, "Well, whatever your crime, they can't incarcerate you for long. Not without a trial by a jury of your peers. Isn't that right, class? Where do we find our right to a trial by our peers?"

The entire class sat glassy eyed and dumbfounded at Van Doorn's swift switch back to the lecture. When she scanned the class for a student willing to answer her questions, she saw Chad still sitting there. "Chad, I think you had better go."

"Oh, right." He grabbed his backpack and headed for the door. He fought the urge to look back at Amy, not wanting to see the rest of the class watching him rush off to his doom with the principal. Head down, he slipped out the door as quietly as he could.

Outside the classroom, he glanced around in a panic. The principal wanted to see him. That was never good. Chad expected he would walk into the office and find Derrick there with accusations of neglect and abuse of his game console. How would he explain this predicament? Would the principal be at all understanding? Chad looked down at his feet. He should hurry down to the office, but he was petrified by the potential for disaster. He noticed his shoes. His mother had scrimped for weeks to be able to buy him some new running shoes for track. Maybe he could just run away. Of course, he knew that would only make things worse, so he headed down the hall toward the administration building.

Chad stepped through the door to the principal's office and was greeted by the perpetually smiling secretary. "Hello, Chad. You can have a seat right there. Mr. Satoro will be with you in a moment." She indicated one of the orange plastic chairs that lined one wall of the waiting room.

He sat, his stomach growing tighter as if it were physically filling with dread. He bent over and rested his chin in his hands, his elbows on his knees. This position gave him a direct view of his running shoes, and he considered again the idea of escape.

#

The whole episode had begun on Monday, as Chad and some friends arrived at their tree, lunches in hand. They found Derrick sitting on the edge of the bench, leaning over a handheld game console. Electronic games, music players, and cellphones were banned from the classrooms and hallways, but they could be used during breaks and during lunch, out of doors. Derrick was so absorbed in his game he seemed unaware of the others as they approached.

"Cool game, Derrick," Chad said when he sat next to him, glancing quickly at the small screen. "Awesome graphics. What is it, a space game?"

"Uh-huh." Derrick grunted, not looking up from the game as his thumbs worked furiously up and down on the glossy black panel.

"I've never seen a game like that before. Where'd you get it?" The graphics were incredible. Chad leaned in closer to watch as Derrick maneuvered a spacecraft through a three-dimensional maze of asteroids and enemy fighter ships. The screen had the definition of the 60-inch UHD TVs Chad had seen at the electronics store, but packed into a four-by-five-inch console.

"My dad brought it home from work. He works at the Andermore Labs, over the hill towards Oakland." he said, as if that somehow explained all mysteries.

"Oh," Chad replied, feigning understanding.

"Do you want to try it?" Derrick asked suddenly.

"Oh, yeah," Chad said, trying to act cool, but unable to hide his enthusiasm. As he reached for the game, the

school bell rang. It was time to head in from lunch.
"Shoot," Chad said, "maybe tomorrow, I guess?"

"Hey," Derrick said, looking at Chad wide-eyed. "Why
don't you take it and play it at home? You can bring it
back in a few days."

"No," Chad said, hesitantly. He thought about how
much fun it would be to play the game, but continued, "I
can't. I don't want to be responsible for something that
expensive. I'll bet it's worth thousands."

Derrick looked around like he was afraid of being
overheard and said as if sharing a secret, "It's no
problem, as long as my dad doesn't find out. He doesn't
know I took it." Derrick grinned at him conspiratorially.
Derrick's father not knowing the game player was gone
worried Chad even more.

"No, I really shouldn't. Besides, I have a ton of
homework to do."

"Come on," Derrick said, anger flashing in his eyes.
"You're not going to break it or lose it." His arguments
were beginning to sound more like threats. "Besides, I
know you're good for it. Just bring it back by Friday."
Derrick pushed the game into Chad's hands.

Chad had expected the device to be warm after running the graphic-intense game, so he was shocked by the coolness of the small box. It felt almost as if it had just been taken from a refrigerator. He couldn't tell if it was made of plastic or metal, and there were no rivets or seams on the shiny black surface.

"No, I'm serious. I can't," Chad's words trailed off. When he looked up from the game player, Derrick was already gone and halfway back to the school. The second bell would ring soon, and he would be late for science if he didn't hurry. He put the game in his lunch bag and ran back to his locker, where he grabbed his backpack. He put the device safely inside one of the inner pockets before heading on to class.

3 - A Big Mistake

The friendly secretary spoke for a moment on her desk phone, then said, "You can go in, Chad. Mr. Satoro is ready for you now."

Chad pushed the door open just enough to slip silently through and stood quietly waiting to be noticed. He really wished he could just melt into the floor and be done with it.

Though middle-aged, the barrel-chested principal looked more like he should be coaching football, or cage fighters, than herding middle school students. He barely glanced up from the papers he was reading to acknowledge Chad's presence.

"Close the door, please, Mr. Baker, and have a seat in that chair." He indicated the seat in front of his desk with a tilt of his head, reading glasses perched on his nose. He returned his gaze to the papers in his hand and scanned them, his bulldog jowls giving his face a perpetual frown.

Sitting, Chad closed his eyes and took a quick breath.

"Do you know what I have here, Mr. Baker?" the principal asked, holding several papers aloft and flipping them slightly at Chad.

Chad shook his head. "No," he said, his voice cracking. When the principal glanced at him, he cleared his throat, and said again, "No, Mr. Satoro."

"It's a report telling me you have won a scholarship for your entry in the school district's creative writing contest. There is a check here for two hundred and fifty dollars, for first place."

"Oh," Chad stammered yet again. He seemed to be stammering a lot today. "Well, um. That's good then, right?" he continued.

"Yes, of course. Very good." Mr. Satoro said, removing his reading glasses. "I wanted to be the first to congratulate you. You have represented our school well. Of course, I will hold onto this check until we present it to you at the end of year assembly next week. You can let your mother know to be there."

"Thank you." They sat staring at one another for several heartbeats, which seemed to Chad like hours.

"That will be all, Mr. Baker. You may go." The principal returned the reading glasses to his nose and shuffled through the stack of papers on his desk.

Chad picked up his backpack and left the office as quickly as he could without knocking anything over. He passed the smiling secretary, waving at her moronically. When the door to the office closed behind him, he leaned against the outer wall, feeling light-headed but relieved.

The bell rang and the halls filled with students hurrying to their lockers or racing to the buses to get the best seats. Chad had time to think, now, since Amy would be in choir for another 45 minutes, unaware of the conflict awaiting her on the baseball field. He loved to hear her sing, whether she was with the choir or by herself. Her voice was clear and pure, and she didn't need music to keep her on key. She always sang with such enthusiasm and confidence; Chad doubted he could ever perform anything in front of a group of people watching, staring, and laughing, without falling apart from fear. The choir would perform at the same assembly where he would be getting his scholarship. By then, everything should be worked out—or he hoped it would be.

He walked toward their lunch tree hoping to come up with a reasonable solution before his meeting with Derrick. He sat on one of the benches below the tree that offered him a view of both the music room and the baseball diamond.

Leaning on his elbow, Chad stared at the dirt at his feet. "This is ridiculous," he said out loud, and tried to convince himself there was really nothing to worry about.

The game player. He took it out of his backpack and turned it over in his hands. He must have done the same thing a thousand times since the first night he had tried to turn it on. Just holding the device made his heart pound in his chest and his stomach roll around with anxiety. He pushed the on/off button—it was more of a circular dark shade of grey in one corner than an actual button. He pushed it several times and looked closely at the screen for any indication the device might function normally, but without success.

"What's up, Chad?"

Startled by Amy's voice so close, he jumped to his feet. He hadn't expected her so soon.

"Amy, you're here," he exclaimed stupidly.

"Yeah, you asked me to meet you here." Her light brown eyes sparkled as she teased him, and she asked, "So, can we talk as we walk home?"

"Well, um, no. Derrick..." he mumbled trying to get his thoughts back together. He hadn't worked out how he would broach the subject and found his mind was now completely blank. "Derrick," he said again, looking at the baseball field and holding up the game player.

Amy looked confused, and concerned as well. She followed Chad's view to the ball field and seeing nothing out of the ordinary, asked, "Chad? Are you okay? What's Derrick got to do with anything?"

"Amy, I'm in trouble," he began and decided it would be best to just run with it. "Derrick thinks I broke his game player and he wants me to pay for it, and I don't have any money."

"Do you need some money? I could ask my dad," she said.

Chad interrupted her. "No, Amy. He doesn't want money. He wants me to give him you."

"That's right, Amy." The deep voice of the older boy broke in. Chad hadn't seen him approach but found he was standing right next to them. "He owes me, and I'm taking you as payment."

Chad fought back his panic. This was all happening too fast. Everything was falling apart like wet toilet paper.

Amy said nothing. She just stared at Derrick, her mouth agape, her face a mask of shock.

"Come on," Derrick commanded, "You're mine now." He turned and headed down a small slope toward the baseball field. Chad gaped as Amy fell in behind without argument.

"Wait, Amy. You don't have to go!" Chad shouted as he ran to catch up to Derrick. "Derrick," he said, and heard the pleading in his own voice, "I can pay you for it. I'll have two hundred and fifty dollars next week. That's enough, isn't it?"

Derrick didn't respond, didn't even look back, he just kept walking with Amy two steps behind him. Her head was bowed, her posture uncharacteristically defeated.

Chad caught back up to Derrick and grabbed him by the arm, turning him. Derrick stopped and pulled his arm from Chad's grasp. He still held the game device in his other hand. "Wait, Derrick, you can't take her. Take your game. I'll pay you for it."

"Keep it. It's garbage. I have what I want," he said dismissively and turned to walk past the first base dugout toward a nature trail that followed along a slow-moving creek.

"Stop!" Chad shouted desperately and grabbed Derrick's arm again.

Derrick spun like a snake striking at a mouse and hit Chad with an upper cut to his jaw. The world lurched crazily as he fell back.

#

When Chad's vision cleared, he found himself lying on his back in the grass along the nature trail, the game device close by, where it had fallen from his hand.

"Amy!" he shouted, getting slowly to his feet. The world spun around him and he leaned against an oak tree, blinking his eyes and wishing his vision would stabilize. "Amy!" he shouted again and rubbed his jaw where Derrick had hit him.

As soon as his legs would hold him, he stumbled down the nature trail, calling for his friend, searching the brush and banks of the creek. Several times he tripped over unseen roots in the shadows under the canopy of oaks. Eventually, he arrived at the street where the nature trail ended. He crossed the creek and ran back along the opposite bank, through the brush and brambles, shouting and looking for where Derrick might have taken her.

Amy was gone.

When he got back to the school, he splashed through the shallow creek and ran up the small slope to the lunch tree. Panting for breath, he sat on the bench as he rubbed the sweat off his forehead and across his short blond hair.

The sun was already behind the school, casting long shadows across the open grassy area to the lunch tree. Chad must have lain in the grass, unconscious, for hours.

"Maybe this is all just a bad joke. Maybe Derrick let her go and she had walked home." It could be true. He should go to her house and check on her.

He picked up his backpack from where it had sat by the bench all afternoon, and headed to the street.

"The Sniders are going to think I'm crazy," he said as he got to the faculty parking lot. "Oh, I know."

He ran back to retrieve the broken game device. Maybe showing it to Amy's parents would lessen how foolish he would look as he tried to explain what happened.

He got to the spot where it had fallen to the ground. He could see the outline of where his body had lain in the tall grass. But, even though he got down on hands and knees and combed through the grass with his fingers, he was unable to find the game player in the fading light.

4 - Facing the Music

Chad walked from the school in the direction of the Sniders' house. How would he face her parents if she wasn't there? How would they react? What would they expect him to know? He wished again this was all a dream. He knew it wasn't.

The sun was below the horizon and it was darkening to full night. Amy's parents would have to have known something was wrong when she didn't come home from school. "She is as regular as clockwork and as predictable as a calendar," her mother had once told Chad when he had stopped by, unexpectedly, to visit. She was smart, too. Her parents would have to know she wouldn't get herself into trouble.

"It would take someone like me to get her this messed up." Chad said as he rounded the corner onto Amy's street.

He expected to see police cars parked in front of the Sniders' house, but there was only one car he could see, at the end of the dark street. It was a black Lincoln

Continental, big and boxy, a style popular before Chad was even born. He recognized the car as a daily feature in the school parking lot. As he walked past it, he glanced sidelong through the windows, but it was empty of occupants.

Amy's house was set back in a large front yard crowded with old trees. Ancient maples, oaks, and sycamores almost completely hid the house from passersby on the street. Most residents of the area believed the land around the house was one of the original homesteads. Many of the trees were estimated at more than one hundred years old, planted in the late eighteen hundreds around the farm house that was removed years ago. The trees formed an opaque ceiling over the walk that led between the massive trunks to the front door. Any light from the stars or moon was effectively shielded as Chad made his way through the darkness, guided by a single light on the Sniders' front porch.

He stood for a moment in front of the door, with his hand raised to knock, steeling his nerves for the inevitable confrontation and interrogation. However, before he could rap his knuckles against the small leaded glass window, the door swung open before him and Mr. Snider stood silhouetted in the doorway.

"Come in, Chad," he said matter-of-factly, his long face and droopy steel grey eyes showing no sign of emotion. "We're in the living room."

Chad's hope bloomed. "Amy is here?" he asked, feeling a sudden wash of relief. As they passed through the kitchen on the way to the living room, Mr. Snider stopped at the refrigerator and poured Chad a glass of ice water.

"No, Chad. She is not," Amy's father said grimly and shook his head. He drew one hand down his hollow cheeks, rubbed his lips with the back of his hand, and continued on to the sitting room.

Chad considered the glass in his hand. His stomach felt as cold and liquid as the water.

He followed Mr. Snider into the living room. As he had guessed, sitting with Mrs. Snider was the owner of the Continental out front, Mrs. Walker. The old woman looked comical and out of place, like a large animated toad sitting human-like in a chair. But what she was doing here, he had no idea. Not once in the two years he had been walking Amy home, had his English teacher come to the Sniders' house. Nor had Amy ever mentioned that her parents knew Mrs. Walker in any significant way.

"Thank you for coming, Chad. Please, have a seat." Mr. Snider's concern was evident on his face. Chad sat on the edge of the couch and sipped from his glass. He looked at Mrs. Snider, who sat straight and proper as she always appeared. Her long neck, mass of dark curls pinned ornately at the top of her head, and the thin, fine bones of her hands folded on her lap gave her the appearance of a Victorian portrait. Her eyes were red-rimmed and puffy, as if she had been crying very recently. Mrs. Walker sat next to her, patting the younger woman's arm, her face the epitome of compassion and understanding. Mrs. Walker looked so sincere Chad wondered if this was, perhaps, a twin sister of his English teacher. He was confident Mrs. Walker didn't have a compassionate cell in her body.

Chad cleared his throat when none of the adults initiated conversation. "Ummm. Did you know I was coming here?"

"I'm sorry, Chad. You must know Amy didn't return home from school today. Typically, you would have been with her, and hours ago. When we saw you approaching the door," Mr. Snider indicated the picture above the mantel of the fire place with a nod of his head, "we assumed you knew something about her absence."

Chad looked above the fireplace. He had sat in this living room countless times and had appreciated and discussed a large print by the Japanese artist, Hiroshige, that hung on the wall above the mantel. The picture was gone. In its place a large monitor displayed several camera views around the house and yard. The bottom left view was from the front porch and showed the entire yard out to the street. They must have known he was on his way to the door from the time he reached Mrs. Walker's car.

"She went with Derrick." Chad launched into his story without preamble. "I told them she didn't have to go. It was my problem, but she acted like she had to go

36

with him and when I tried to stop him he hit me." He stared at the floor and rubbed his bruised jaw. He wanted to look Amy's parents in the face, to see the expression in their eyes—to see if they understood—but he felt so terribly ashamed.

"When I woke up, they were gone. Derrick's game was there, but when I went back for it later, I couldn't find it. I looked for Amy and Derrick. They were headed toward the nature trail, but I couldn't find them, either. They were just gone."

He stood, his hands held out as if pleading with the three adults for mercy, struggling to find the words to express the depth of his guilt. He gave up, turned to Amy's mother, and said, "I'm sorry. It's all my fault. Derrick took her somewhere and I don't know how to find her."

"Chad," Mr. Snider was suddenly there, standing beside him, his hand on Chad's shoulder. "It's really not your fault. You don't know everything that is going on. You're Amy's friend, and that is important. But, we're missing parts of your story. Could you go to the beginning and slowly tell us all that happened, so we can figure out how to get her back?"

Chad looked up at the tall man. His own father had disappeared shortly after Chad's birth. With no grandfathers or uncles in his life, Chad's closest adult male role model was his brother, who was currently away serving in the military. Amy's father spoke with such understanding and tenderness Chad felt safe in this home. He could trust Amy's parents.

But then he thought of Mrs. Walker. For the first time since entering, he looked at her closely. There, cradled on her lap was Derrick's game device. He looked from the black cube to the English teacher's eyes. She returned his gaze and nodded. "Yes, Chad. Please, sit back down and tell us everything you know. Anything you remember."

Chad was amazed at the absence of sarcasm and condescension in her voice and demeanor. He looked from person to person, then sat back down and launched into the story again.

He spoke about Derrick and how he seemed to arrive from nowhere. As he described the game player, Mrs.

Walker examined it, turning it over in her hands several times. He spoke of the events, but also the emotions he felt, in as much depth and detail as he could remember. At times new details came to him, and to his chagrin, he told them of his feelings for Amy to a degree he hadn't intended.

"I saw her walking away, behind Derrick like she was trapped or defeated," Chad said, "and I knew I had done something terrible, and something terrible was going to happen to Amy. I couldn't stand it, I couldn't let her go. But then he hit me, and I was out like a light."

He stood again and paced around in circles. "I don't know what I'm saying. Does any of this make any sense?" He looked around hopelessly. The shattered expression on Mrs. Snider's face magnified his feelings of guilt and he sat back down with his head in his hands.

Mrs. Walker spoke. "This boy Derrick. Do you know his last name?"

"No, I'm sorry, I just never..." he trailed off.

"Don't worry, Chad," she said. "You're not on trial here. You have done nothing wrong. We just need to gather all the information we can, so we can get Amy back. Now, can you think of a time in the last week when you were talking with Derrick in the hallways, the library, or the cafeteria?"

Chad thought. "Yeah. The day after he gave me the game player, before school started we talked in the library."

The teacher's eyes lit up. "Good. Good," she said and looked back and forth between Amy's parents as if for confirmation. "I should be able to find him on video from one of the library's cameras. Chad, will you please meet me at the school around noon tomorrow, after I have had a chance to review the video?"

Still wary of the sudden and dramatic change in his dreaded English teacher, he nodded his head. "Sure, yeah. I want to help fix this."

Music suddenly began to play from inside his backpack. "Oh, shoot. My mom." He rummaged through the backpack to get the phone before it went to voice mail. It was his brother's old phone, because his mother couldn't afford one for Chad. When Mike's National Guard unit was deployed to Afghanistan, he figured he wouldn't get much use out of it over there, so he left if for Chad. Chad didn't use it much, only to communicate with his mother—which he had completely forgotten to do.

He answered the phone, trying to sound casual. "Mom, I'm sorry, I'm at Amy's house. We got busy and I forgot to call." He paused as his mother asked if he and Amy were there alone. "No, her parents are here. Do you want to talk to them?" His mother declined, but said it was time for him to be getting home. "Okay. I'll be home in a few minutes."

Mr. Snider stood when Chad did, and stopped Chad on the way to the door. "Let me give you a ride home. We can talk a bit more in the car."

As soon as they were driving away from the house, Mr. Snider started right in.

"I'm sure you have dozens of questions for me. The short version is this: Amy is not an ordinary girl. She is not even from here, from this world. We have been hiding her here. You might say we have been trying to hide her in plain sight. But, things were going too smoothly, and we should have known better.

"From your own words, it's clear you have developed an emotional bond with Amy. A stronger bond than we could have expected. Had we known of the connection, we would have brought you into our confidence, to help protect the both of you."

Chad struggled to keep up with Mr. Snider's dialog.

"Emotional connection? It's not like we're in love or anything," he said defensively.

"Boys your age become infatuated easily. It's called puppy love, and it usually passes quickly. But you must have surpassed that level and moved on to a more real or permanent attachment or you wouldn't have been able to give her away to Derrick and transfer that connection to him. Amy could only be betrayed by someone who loved her."

"Betrayed," Chad said aghast. "I didn't know. I'm so sorry."

They reached Chad's house. Mr. Snider stopped the car and turned off the engine.

"No, Chad. There is no time for sorry, and it wouldn't do any good anyway. It was your love for Amy that made it possible for Derrick to take her away. Since it was you who released her to Derrick, also, only you can go and bring her back."

5 - The Missing Culprit

"Hi, Mom," Chad said when he closed and locked the front door.

"Hi, sweetheart." She looked up from the text book she was studying in the kitchen, and brushed back her straight blond hair with the fingers of her left hand before hooking it behind her ear. Her deep blue eyes were tired. Though she had been unemployed for several months, she still worked a long day—following job leads in the morning, taking classes at the community college and studying late into the night.

"Are you hungry? I can make you something to eat," she said and made as if to stand.

"No thanks, Mom. I'm really not that hungry," he said. "I'm tired. I think I'll just go to bed."

Before he could leave the kitchen, his mother exclaimed, "Bed? On a Friday night? It's only nine o'clock. Don't you want to go do something with your friends?"

"Not really. I just want to go to bed," he said and tried to smooth his hair back. He remembered how filthy he must be and thought about taking a shower. As he turned toward the hallway, he stopped. "Besides, Mrs. Walker wants me to meet her at the school at noon tomorrow."

"Mrs. Walker? Your English teacher? On a Saturday?" She shook her head and her hair slipped from behind her ear to hang straight down along her face. "I thought you were doing well in English."

"I am. In fact, Mr. Satoro told me today I won a two-hundred-and-fifty-dollar prize for a story I wrote."

"That's wonderful!" She stepped over and hugged Chad from behind then leaned her head over and rested her cheek on the top of his head. He was nearly as tall as she now.

"You'll have to think carefully about how you want to spend it."

If I ever get it, he thought to himself.

His mother stepped back, turned Chad around and looked closely at him. She noticed the dirt on his face and reached up to lightly touch the swollen redness on his jaw. "What happened to you today?"

He shook his head and looked at the floor. "I've had a really tough day. Can I just tell you about it in the morning?"

She obviously wanted to ask more questions, but said instead, "Okay, Chad. If that's what you need."

"Thanks, Mom. I'll tell you everything in the morning." He walked to the bathroom to shower before getting into bed.

#

Chad didn't sleep much that night. His thoughts jumped spasmodically between images of Amy sitting in class, singing with the school choir, and talking with their circle of friends at the lunch tree. Then Derrick would appear, leering over them, his black eyes suddenly flashing with anger. No matter how Chad tried to control his thoughts, to relax his mind and think of something pleasant, the images continually returned to

Derrick leading Amy away, her head down and shoulders rounded.

When he did finally sleep, he slept so soundly that when he awoke, he only vaguely remembered dreams of Amy deep in a cave or dungeon. She wasn't chained or miserable. She stood defiant and argued with someone, though Chad didn't know if she argued with someone unseen, or with him. He lay in his bed and stared at the ceiling, trying to remember more details of the quickly fading dream.

His mother's voice called from the hallway, "Chad, honey. It's after eleven. I thought you had to be at the school by noon."

"Thanks, Mom, I'm getting up."

He walked out to the kitchen in his pajamas. "I can't find my jeans. Did you see them?"

"Yes, I took them from your room. I was doing some laundry and thought you might want them washed."

He watched her face as she spoke, feeling there was something his mother was holding back. Her eyes clearly showed her concern. "What's the matter, Mom?"

She brought a gallon of milk from the refrigerator and placed it on the table. "You'd better eat some cereal, it's getting late. While you're eating, maybe you can tell me about this note. I found it in your pocket."

In her hand she held the note he had written in science class the day before.

"Did you read it?" Chad asked, though he already knew what the answer would be.

She nodded her head.

"Mom, I know this sounds crazy, but some crazy things have happened to me. I waited to talk to Amy after school and thought when she met me she would just tell me I was stupid and tell Derrick to take his game and get lost. She didn't. Derrick told her she belonged to him and she had to go with him."

His voice sounded high and whiny in his own ears. "She just went with him, like she was a runaway dog who'd been caught by her master. When I tried to stop him, Derrick hit me. He hit me hard, too. I was out for a while.

"The weirdest part was when I went to Amy's house to see if she had just gone home. When I told her parents, they acted like they knew this kind of thing might happen. Sure, they were upset, but they weren't freaking out. On top of that, Mrs. Walker was at their house, and acted like she was part of a conspiracy, or the CIA or something."

He finally poured some cereal into the bowl, eating quickly and talking around mouthfuls. "Mrs. Walker had Derrick's game player and kept messing with it while we talked. She must have picked it up while I was running around looking for Amy. She wants me to meet her at the school to see if we can identify Derrick on the security camera footage."

Chad's mother sat and stared at her son—not at him, really, but through him. He looked down, uncomfortable with her silence, and continued, "The worst part is, they say I am the one who needs to go get her back, since I'm the one who sent her away."

He tried to figure out a way to explain his emotional attachment to Amy, but couldn't understand it himself, so he let it drop for now.

"Go get her?" His mother sounded a little frantic. "This isn't one of your fantasy stories, though it does sound fantastic. This is the real world, Chad. Kids don't run off and rescue abducted kids. This is a job for adults, specifically the police. Hurry up and finish your cereal while I get my car keys. I'm going with you to the school and have a talk with Mrs. Walker myself."

"Okay," Chad said, relieved to have her along. His mother was smart and logical. If anyone could figure this out, she could.

He carried his backpack to the kitchen and started looking through the cupboards.

"What are you doing?" His mother followed and stood behind him.

He took out a package of fig bars and slipped them into his pack. "I know I didn't do much in the boy scouts, but I do want to be prepared. I don't know how long it will take to get Amy back, but if I have to go, I don't want to get too hungry. Or thirsty." Chad added some bottles of water.

His mother crossed her arms. "I'm not going to let them make you go, Chad."

"They're not going to *make* me go. Amy is my friend, my best friend. If there is anything I can do to help, I want to do it."

"We'll see about that." His mother scowled. "Come on. Let's get this done."

#

They arrived at the school well before noon. Only two other cars sat in the parking lot—Mrs. Walker's Continental, and the Sniders' minivan.

The glass door to the administration office stood open. Mr. and Mrs. Snider waited inside where they could watch Chad and his mother approach. Mr. Snider stood as they walked through the door.

"Chad, Mrs. Baker. Thanks for coming," Mr. Snider said with a small, grim nod. His bushy black eyebrows formed a bold V as he frowned. He patted Chad on the back and walked past them to lock the door. Amy's father didn't seem at all surprised Chad's mother had come.

"Come on back," he said after shaking the door to make sure it had locked, then led them down a hallway to a small, dark room. Mrs. Walker looked up as they all crowded into the security office. Ten monitors filled one wall, though only three of them were on.

She nodded to Mrs. Baker in greeting and then pointed at one of the monitors. "Look here, Chad. Here you are with a group of friends. Is Derrick one of these boys?"

"No. He had already left when those guys were talking with me."

Mrs. Walker ran the recording rapidly in reverse for a few minutes. Chad watched the comical scene as the boys flapped their hands and arms and then walked away backwards. There was a flicker of static and Chad walked away, backwards, himself.

He shook his head and turned to his English teacher. "Wait a minute. He followed me into the library. I talked with him, right there where you saw me. He walked away and my friends walked up. He was there, but he's not in the video?"

6 - Get Ready, Get Set

Mrs. Walker ran the video forward again, but in slow motion.

They watched the monitor view from above, looking down on Chad's head as he walked onto the screen and stopped. He waved his hands and bobbed his head as if he spoke with someone, though there was no one within a normal conversational distance. A hazy patch in front of him flashed static a few times. When the haziness cleared, Chad's friends approached. They spoke together for a few minutes and all walked away.

"Hmm, I might have guessed." Mrs. Walker said and looked at Amy's dad, who nodded his head in agreement.

She reversed the video again, past the point where Chad first walked in. Then she entered some commands on the keyboard and recorded the portion where Chad talked with the hazy patch. Copying the recorded piece to a USB drive, she plugged it into a laptop set up next to the other keyboard. Mrs. Walker started a program on the laptop and opened the file from the USB.

While Chad's teacher worked, Mr. Snider pulled some chairs into the room, offering one to Chad's mother. She sat with a view of the monitor, Chad standing behind her.

"Oh, Mom. That's the game player Derrick gave me," Chuck said pointing to the small black box sitting next to the laptop where Mrs. Walker worked.

His teacher looked up, a smile lighting her normally stony face. "Yes. I have something to show you about that, in a moment. But first, let's see what this video will reveal."

She typed some commands on the keyboard and waited while the video processed. In the middle of the laptop's screen a progress bar slowly crept toward completion. When the bar reached the end and blinked off, Chad's image appeared. He stood under the security camera in the library. Every few seconds the image refreshed as time elapsed slowly in the video. Suddenly, standing next to Chad on the screen, was a tall, pale, dark-haired boy.

"That's him!" Chad shouted, then felt sheepish for making such an exclamation in the small room. Images of Derrick clicked past on the video, one by one. At one point, Derrick looked up, directly into the camera. The next image showed only his back as he turned away. Mrs. Walker reversed the video until she held the boy's image on the screen.

"Thank you, Chad. He doesn't look familiar to me. How about you, Ted? Miriam? No, I didn't think so. Well, let me load his image and run some checks."

She dragged the cursor across the screen to highlight Derrick's head and shoulders, copying the image and opening another program on the laptop. She pasted Derrick's image into an empty box and clicked the run button.

The picture of Derrick blurred as image after image of other people was overlaid on his in rapid succession. Measurements and calculations continuously ran across the bottom of the screen. When the overlays stopped, a red progress bar moved across the bottom of the screen. As it reached 100%, Derrick's face disappeared, and the words, "no exact match" appeared in large letters.

"Of course, they wouldn't send a known operative. Especially since there aren't many the right age. I'll look for a family match." Mrs. Walker entered a few new commands.

A table appeared quickly on the screen with numbers filling the columns and rows as the program ran. Calculations scrolled past. When the data screen finally came to a halt, the bottom line read, "95% probability match: Rossanour family genetics".

"Hmmm," Mrs. Walker said, turning in her chair to look up at Chad. She wore her calculating expression, which often warned the children in her class she was about to make an acidic observation at a student's expense. She stared at Chad long enough to make him nervous. Was she waiting for him to say something? The wrinkles around her eyes and across her forehead seemed to deepen with each passing moment. But then she turned her gaze on his mother. Without a word, the older woman nodded and turned back to the laptop. She opened the previous screen where Derrick and Chad both stood. She highlighted Chad's head and shoulders, copied and pasted the image into the second program as she had done with Derrick's image, straight into the family genetics query.

The program ran its routine of overlaying images on Chad's picture. A table appeared on the screen, and a smug grin spread across Mrs. Walker's face as she looked away from the computer. "Just as I suspected."

The table read: Eyes, 100%, Nose, 98%, Mouth, 100%, Ears, 97%. Overall, 98% probability match, Lorantelle family genetics.

"You know, it figures," she said looking first at the Sniders then to Chad's mother. "With this amount of Lorantelle genetics, either you or Chad's father must be one. What is your maiden name, Mrs. Baker?" Mrs. Walker pierced Chad's mother with one of her sharpest glares.

Mrs. Baker sat up straight in her chair, arms crossed. After a long moment, she said, "It's Baker. I never took his father's name."

"What was his last name? What happened to him?"

"Lawrence. He said his name was Steven Lawrence. I never had any cause not to believe him." She dropped her hands back into her lap and slumped her shoulders.

Chad's mother shook her head and looked the older woman in the eyes. "I don't know what happened to him." She looked back down at her hands. "When I told Steven I had gotten pregnant, he became moody. After a while, he was irritable all the time. At first, I tried talking with him about it, but it would just make him angrier. He would blow up at the drop of a hat and storm around the house, ranting. I never understood what made him so angry. After a while, I stopped asking.

"Once Chad was born, Steven started sleeping in another room on the nights he came home late from work. One day, he didn't come home at all. He didn't call or anything. I never saw him again. I assumed he had just walked out on Chad and me. I never thought about calling the police until months later, when I went to legal services to find out how to get a divorce. They asked me for a copy of the missing persons report. I told them I had left it at home, and I would bring it in the following week. I was so embarrassed I never went back."

She closed her eyes and shook her head. "I was so bitter back then, about the neglect and isolation. I had just had a baby. It never occurred to me something may have actually happened to him."

"Did you ever meet his family?" Mrs. Snider asked.

"No. He told me he was an only child and his parents were gone. We never spoke much about it. If I pressed him too hard, he would get cagey and irritable."

Mrs. Walker listened quietly while Chad's mother spoke. She dabbed at her eyes with a tissue and said, "My Jack was a Lorantelle as well. I miss him still. Well, anyway, your husband disappeared, what, thirteen years ago?"

"Yes, he did."

Mrs. Walker got to her feet and held out the small black box for the others to see. Like someone flipped a switch, her look of concern changed to a grin. She pointed to the writing scrolled across the small screen. Below, at the bottom of the box, a small red light slowly flashed. "If I understand this correctly, you have maybe

30 minutes to find the gateway and cross before it closes. That's not a lot of time."

Chad's mother opened her mouth as if to ask a question, but closed it again and frowned.

Mrs. Walker said, as if explaining the obvious, "When it closes, we may not find the right gate again. Opening another would cost us a lot of time. Chad, what do you have in your backpack?"

He shook himself like he was coming awake from a confusing dream and began shuffling through his backpack. "Umm, my phone, a wind breaker, an extra sweatshirt, fig bars, granola bars, some bottles of water. Why, do you need something?"

Mrs. Walker's expression was serious and uncompromising. "No. I'm glad you thought ahead. You need to get going right now and it may be a day or more before we can get some of our people to meet up with you with provisions."

Chad's mother stood up, "Go? Where do you think he is going?"

"Mom, I'm sorry. But I have to go," Chad reached out and touched her lightly on the arm. She looked so frail and small next to Mr. Snider. His mother had, no doubt, skipped a few meals to make ends meet for their family. But only when he laid his hand on her slender arm and looked at her weary face and hollow cheeks, did Chad realize how many dinners she must have missed.

"It's my fault Derrick was able to take Amy," Chad said, his voice quivering with anxiety and adrenaline.

"No." His mother shook her head. Her voice had a note of pleading to it when she said, "Mr. Snider said it wasn't your fault. Besides, Derrick tricked you. You aren't responsible."

"I don't know what I'm getting into," Chad said and held his hand up to forestall any argument, "but I know this. Amy is my friend. I trust her. I know if she told me I needed to jump out of the window and fly to the moon, I would, and I could. She wouldn't ask me to do something if it wasn't necessary."

He gave his mother a chance to speak. When she didn't, he said, "But she's not here, and she can't ask me. So, I have to trust her parents. I do trust them, Mom. Because of you."

"Me?" She sounded shocked.

"Yes. You taught me to be honest and always tell the truth. You wouldn't expect anything of me without expecting it of yourself. I have to believe Amy's parents are the same way, because I know Amy." He nodded to them and raised his eyebrows. She stared at him sternly at first, then softened. She looked at the ground at her feet.

She embraced him suddenly. "Chad. You don't even know where you will be going, or how you will get back."

Then she stepped back, but held onto his shoulders, "You have to come back, as quickly as possible. Mike..."

"Mike will be back soon, probably." Chad wondered how he could say that. His brother was in Afghanistan. He led patrols through the countryside. For him, every day held a risk of death.

Mrs. Walker stepped up and said, "We need to hurry. Come with me." They hustled back out of the school they way they'd come in.

At the front door, Mrs. Baker confronted Amy's father. "So how is he supposed to find your daughter, and how does he get back?"

"Here is as much as I know." Amy's father spoke rapidly, looking at Chad. "The world you are going to is very similar to this one. The people there have passed back and forth from the dimensions to this world for more than a thousand years. The box is a key that will get you through the first transition. It may get you through more, but you may need to find more keys along the way. You will have to make several transitions before you are able to return. Each transition takes you into another dimension.

"We don't know if Derrick left the box behind by mistake, or if he left it on purpose. It may help you learn vital information, or it may give you away. Until you find someone to teach you more about it, use it sparingly.

"Once you cross over, people who are working with us will know you are there. They should already know Amy is there. They will search you out to aid you. Just be careful about who you trust, because it will be very hard to tell friend from foe."

Head spinning as he tried to process everything, Chad slung his backpack off his shoulder and began digging inside it. "Mom, here's Mike's phone. You may need it." Chad started to hand the phone to his mother.

"No, Chad, hold onto it," Mr. Snider said. "Remember, our worlds are very similar and very close together. You may be able to use the phone there, or possibly contact us here in this dimension. Now, you and your mother get down to the ball field. Wait only a minute, and if I haven't caught up with you, find the gateway. I need to check one thing." Mr. Snider shared a knowing glance with Mrs. Walker.

"But, how will I find the gateway?" Chad asked. "I ran the entire length of the nature trail yesterday, before I came to your house."

"Hold the key in front of you. It should make the gate appear. You weren't holding it yesterday when you were looking for Amy, which is why you didn't spot it then. Now go."

As Chad took his mother's hand to pull her along with him, he heard Mrs. Walker say, "Well, we have the Lorantelles involved. That gives me hope."

Chad didn't know if she spoke to him or to herself. Regardless, the woman's declaration gave him hope as well.

7 - Don't Bother Knocking

Chad and his mother stood between the first base dugout and the nature trail that followed the creek through the oak trees. He held the black box in front of him, looking from its screen to the trees ahead.

"This is so crazy. It's right there in front of us. It's right there, Mom. Can't you see it?" Chad was trying to convince his mother as Amy's dad ran up behind them.

"She can't see it, Chad. She's not holding the key," he told them, slightly out of breath. "You have to hold the box to be able to see the gateway."

"Here, Mom. Take a look." Chad shoved the game player into her hands, pointing into the trees.

Mrs. Baker's eyes widened as she pointed the key toward the right area. "Oh. It is there. No wait. Sorry, it's back."

She turned to Mr. Snider and continued, "It disappeared for a moment, but now it's back." The small red light at the bottom of the box had faded, though it flashed on and off more rapidly than before.

"That's not good. Chad, you need to go now." Mr. Snider took the box from Mrs. Baker's hands and shoved it back into Chad's.

"No, wait. Don't go, Chad. We can figure something else out." His mother was frantic and angry. She was crying. The tears on her face stabbed him in the heart. She would be completely alone now. Mike was in Afghanistan and Chad—who knew where he would end up?

Mrs. Snider spoke for the first time since arriving at the ball field. "Please, Mrs. Baker, we need him to go. It's not just for Amy. There is more going on that we don't have the time to go into right now."

Chad looked toward the oak trees. He felt guilty putting his or Amy's needs over those of his mother. While he battled with these emotions, the gateway disappeared. Everything faded from his hearing as he panicked.

The gateway flickered back into view, was gone, and then back again. He didn't wait another second, but ran headlong at the gateway. He vaguely heard his mother shout his name before he was through. He looked behind him and for an instant the scene became like a movie theater with him sitting in the darkness of the back row, the glowing screen before him a window to another world.

Suddenly, the view of Amy's parents and his mother worriedly searching the trees disappeared and Chad was left alone in the darkness.

The pitch blackness reminded him of when he had gone with his Cub Scout pack to a cave in the Sierra Nevada foothills. During the tour, their guide turned off the lights to show the kids what absolute darkness was.

He scuffed his feet and felt dirt and grass under the soles of his running shoes. He closed his eyes and listened. Laughing at himself he said out loud, "That was dumb. I really don't need to close my eyes. It's dark enough already."

His voice didn't echo like it would in a large cavern or an empty room, though the darkness felt heavy and seemed to press in on him. When he listened closely he could hear the soft gurgling of a creek. If it wasn't the creek that ran along the school, then there was another one just like it on this side of the gateway.

Chill, damp air quickly penetrated his t-shirt. Chad tugged the light jacket from his backpack and pulled it on, though he left it unzipped.

He slowly turned in a circle, carefully listening for other sounds. There were none—no birds chirping or insects buzzing past. No people sounds either. At the school he could always hear cars driving past on the street close by.

As he turned, the box in his hands suddenly warmed and cooled again. He looked toward the box in the utter blackness and was surprised to find a small red bar had replaced the flashing dot which had warned of the portal's closure.

The glowing bar gave off just enough light for Chad to see the sides of his thumbs as he held the box. The bar moved from right to left as Chad shifted his body from left to right. As the bar passed the center of the device's screen the box noticeably warmed in his hands, and then cooled as the bar moved onward to the edge of the screen.

With the bar centered and the box warm in his hands the burbling creek was to his right as it had been when he entered the gateway. Chad assumed the box was telling to move forward in this direction. But if he followed its direction where would it take him? Farther into the darkness?

Unsure what to do, Chad sat down where he was. He could feel the dry dirt of a trail underneath him and the short grass off to the sides. He felt funny sitting in the middle of what was obviously a path. Something could come rushing past and trip over him; or trample him, for that matter. He held the device in one hand and felt around through the grass to the side of the path to ensure there was adequate sitting space, and moved well off the dirt and away from the creek. As he felt around he found the occasional dry leaf, but no major obstruction prevented him from sitting cross legged in the short grass to think.

He reviewed what he knew. The game device may or may not have been left intentionally, so he couldn't trust it. The box was a key to the gateway he had just passed through, and now it was telling him which direction it wanted him to go.

Mr. Snider had told him he would have to pass through a number of gateways, each one taking him to another dimension. Each gateway would need a key. Mrs. Walker had also told Chad to use the box sparingly.

Therefore, his choices were: remain where he was and wait for something to happen, such as a key appearing or a helpful stranger walking up with a flashlight; or follow the directions of the questionable box and walk blindly into the darkness. He wished he could ask someone for advice.

"Wait a minute. I can," he said and felt through his backpack for the cellphone. Logically, his mother and the Sniders were only feet away, though in another dimension. Perhaps they had left already, but it wasn't likely. Chad was sure his mother was still standing in the spot where he had left her, arguing with the Sniders. She was a strong-willed woman and Chad knew she wouldn't accept anything they said as a given.

He felt along the edges of the phone until he found the power button. The face lit up enough for Chad to see his hands. He turned it over toward the ground, but the light was far too weak to reach more than a few inches.

He wished it had a flashlight app like newer phones, but wishing wasn't going to get him anywhere at the moment.

A small hourglass spun in a circle as the phone searched for a network signal. Within seconds four signal bars lit up, showing a strong connection. Chad quickly punched in his mother's phone number and waited as it rang once, twice, and, "Chad?" his mother asked, clearly astonished.

"Yeah, Mom, it's me. I've crossed over. Did you see me go?"

"Yes. We just watched you run into the trees and then... Then you were gone." Her voice trailed off. She sounded desolate and Chad felt renewed guilt at leaving her all alone.

"Chad, you've got to come back. Now."

"Sorry, Mom. The gate closed behind me. I couldn't come back right now if I wanted to." He said it with much more confidence than he felt. "I was just testing the phone to see if it would work from here. Oh, could you tell Mr. Snider it's pitch dark here? I can't see a thing. But I think the box is telling me which way to go. Should I follow it?"

Chad heard his mother repeat his words to Amy's dad, not removing the phone from her mouth. She said, obviously speaking to Mr. Snider, "What do you mean he has no other choice?" A pause. "Be careful? That's your best advice?"

She sounded hysterical, but who wouldn't? His mother had just seen her son disappear in front of her eyes, and now he was speaking to her on the phone like he was just down the street.

"Mom. I'm sorry. I have to go. I don't want to burn up the battery. I'll text you when I know something. Feel free to text me too. I'll check a couple times a day to see if you sent anything. I love you, Mom. Stick close to the Sniders. We all need to work together. I love you." His mother started to reply but Chad ended the call and shut off the phone. He was afraid if she started talking, she wouldn't stop and let him go.

"Follow the box and be careful. Not a lot to go on."

Steeling his nerves, he got to his feet.

8 - Insight

Chad turned back and forth slowly to get a feel for the sensitivity and accuracy of the box. When he was confident he could maintain the red bar in the center of the screen—the warmth from the box gave him additional feedback—he stepped forward.

Almost immediately, he stopped and checked the time on his watch, then lifted the box directly in front of him again. He shuffled onward blindly. The glowing red bar shifted back and forth slightly with each step.

The cold darkness was almost tangible. He pushed through it like a man wading against the current of a river. The darkness pushed against his body and tugged at his clothes as it passed.

Chad tried lowering the box to waist level, to rest his arms, but quickly found himself stepping off the trail into the grass, making sharp turns to correct his direction. Only when the box was held out at arm's length did he stay on the meandering dirt path. The single sound besides his footfalls and his breathing was the creek to his right. At times he could hear it splashing against its banks only a few feet from the path. Other times its babbling sounded quite distant.

He continued this way for some time until his arms were too tired to hold up. Collapsing in the grass to the side of the trail, he drank one of his bottles of water. He checked the time, expecting to find hours had passed during his blind travel through the darkness. According to his watch he had been walking for just a few minutes. Stupid thing must be broken, he thought, and finished off the water.

He returned the empty bottle to his pack so he would be able to refill it later, then leaned back on his hands and looked around himself.

While he walked he'd kept his eyes focused on the display of the game device. Having to keep the red bar in the device's center, he hadn't been conscious of the darkness around him. Now, as he rested, he had the sense the sky directly above was a slightly lighter shade of black. He held his hand between his face and the sky and could just barely perceive its outline. He stood again and looked around himself some more. If he relaxed his eyes and didn't try too hard, he could make out the vague line where the sky met the horizon. Turning in slow circles, he found nothing obscured the flat edge of horizon, like he was standing in the center of a barren plain.

Optimism flared in him at the thought of the sunrise. He wouldn't be wandering in darkness much longer. "Still wandering, just not in the dark," Chad said and was startled to hear his own voice break the silence.

Rested, his arms much less leaden, he was ready to be on his way. Though it was still too dark to see shapes as more than shadows in the night, he strode forward under the guidance of the small box.

As he continued along the path, the sky seemed to lighten almost with every step. The dome of pale light overhead eventually reached a shade of gray equal to that of an overcast November—enough light to clearly see his surroundings but not so much as to cast a good shadow. The distinct track in the short grass meandered forward into the distant gloom, and he kept to it with only an occasional glance at the box to confirm he was still headed in the correct direction.

He checked his watch again and decided it truly was broken. According to the watch, only an hour had passed since he'd come into this world.

With the arrival of dawn, Chad could see the plain he stood upon was not entirely barren. The path he walked roughly followed the course of the creek to his right, though he walked in the opposite direction of its flow. The ground climbed marginally from both sides of the creek and ahead of him. Carpeted with short new grass, small hills and vales spread out from him in all directions. Only the occasional gnarled oak tree broke up the horizon line. The dips and hollows were shrouded in mist, a gray reflection of the grim sky above.

Weary again, Chad sat on the cold dirt of the path to rest. Mist had collected on the grass and it was quite wet. He drank some more water and ate one of the granola bars.

He got out the phone and turned it on. There were no waiting text messages.

He typed, *It's finally light here now. Can see where I'm going.*

He sent the message and was about to turn off the phone when he noticed the time on it matched the time on his watch. He shut the phone off and shook his head. "I'll worry about what that means later."

Rested, Chad rubbed the sleeves of his jacket to shake off the chill and returned to the path. The trail continued in a meandering yet direct route forward, and he rarely felt it necessary to consult the game player to ensure it and the path were still in agreement.

After what seemed like hours of walking, in the far distance, perhaps miles away, Chad could see a change in the horizon. At first there appeared to be only a line of trees, but as he got closer it became clear he was approaching an oak forest.

He followed the trail to the edge of the forest. The creek cleaved the ancient oaks as far as he could see, and ran side by side with the trail. He consulted the black box which confirmed Chad's, or the box's, destination followed the path through the oaks.

Mechanically, Chad looked at his watch again, and sighed.

"How long will it take me to remember this thing is broken?"

Strangely comforted to hear his own voice in the vast, soundless landscape, he continued a one-sided dialog. "Well, if my watch is correct, I've been walking through this world for less than 2 hours. Instead, I feel like I've walked half a night and most of a day."

He pulled the backpack from his shoulders and carried it with one hand as he stepped from the trail to walk to the edge of the creek. He stared down into the clear water. "I wonder if this water is okay to drink. I only have half of a bottle left."

Chad was startled when a soft feminine voice spoke from behind him. "You're lost, aren't you?"

He dropped his backpack and spun around to see who had addressed him. There was no one. He searched the giant gray oaks but wasn't able to find the source of the voice.

"This is great. First I'm talking to myself, then I hear voices, and now I'm talking to myself again. What's next?"

He turned back to the stream and retrieved his backpack. He slung it back onto his shoulders, consulted the black box to confirm his destination still lay within the oak woods, and turned back to the trail.

In the middle of the dirt path, between where Chad stood and the dense oak forest, sat a small gray, short-haired cat. Its fur was the color of slate—the paws, ears, and tail frosted with silver. Its bright eyes shone like new copper pennies.

Chad approached the cat cautiously and stopped a few yards away. He expected it to run away. Instead it calmly looked at him, occasionally twitching its tail.

Chad spoke to the cat, "You're the only creature I have seen since I came to this place. Makes me wonder if you're real at all."

The cat got to its feet and casually walked the short distance to where Chad stood and rubbed its body against his leg. It felt real enough. Its small body felt surprisingly warm through his blue jeans as it pressed against his calf. As it did so, Chad felt the black box in his hands suddenly go as cold as the dismal day around him. He looked at the box. The red direction bar was gone. As he stood facing down the trail toward the oak forest, the red bar should have been centered on the screen. He turned rapidly to the left and the right, but the bar didn't return.

"You can put that thing away now. It won't work while I'm around." The cat looked at Chad. The voice was the same one he had just heard, and came from the direction of the cat. "That's right. I'm speaking to you. I'm serious, too. You don't want to follow that box from here. We need to go a different direction now."

The cat walked to the edge of the stream, turned to Chad where he stood on the trail, and said, "Pick me up, please. We need to cross the stream and I don't want to get my paws wet."

Chad shook his head. "I don't believe it. A cat is talking to me, and it's not even moving its mouth."

"Listen," the cat said and hesitated. "What's your name?" she asked.

"I'm Chad," he replied with caution. "But, if you're here to guide me, why don't you know my name? And how do I know you're on the right side?"

"I'm not psychic," she replied matter-of-factly. "And how do you know *you're* on the right side?"

Chad shook his head in surprise. "I don't know how I know, but I am. I'm here to help a friend who got kidnapped. She's never hurt anyone, so whoever took her must be bad."

"There are flaws in that logic," the cat said. "You'll need to work that out on your own. You'll have plenty of time, later."

The cat walked to the edge of the creek before she spoke again. "I can tell you this much. The trail you were on follows the creek into the oak woods. It's an old forest, with old and unusual creatures. If you followed the trail, you would never reach its end, and it is unlikely you would ever find your way back out."

"I don't know..."

"I can see that," the cat said with an audible sigh. "You can come with me and get out of this place, or you can go back and follow the trail. The choice is yours. But, if you want to help your friend, you need to follow me, and get on with it."

Chad looked back at the trail into the forest, at the cat at his feet, and then at the game player still in his hands.

"How am I supposed to know what to do?" he asked her, but she only shrugged.

"Okay then, let's go. At least you'll be someone to talk to," Chad said and picked up the cat.

9 - Finding Understanding

Chad walked to the edge of the creek and put the cat back down. He sat and took off his shoes and socks, put them in his pack, slung it over his shoulders, and bent to pick up the cat. After scouting out the best place to try to cross, he stepped into the water. It was unexpectedly cold, ice cold, and he hissed as his feet and calves cramped almost immediately. The slow-moving water lapped at his knees and blue jeans where they had slipped back down his legs as he walked. He stepped timidly and carefully through the coarse gravel, grateful there weren't any large mossy rocks where he might slip and fall completely into the freezing creek.

Soon he was on the opposite bank, where he sat in the grass again and waited a few minutes while the water dried from his legs. The cat padded from where Chad had placed her on the ground, and licked water from his calves.

"Is this water okay to drink?" he asked the cat.

"Of course. Why wouldn't it be?" He couldn't see any expression on her face—though it was clear from her inflection she was incredulous.

"Well, I don't know," he said, embarrassed. "I'm not from around here, you know. And back where I'm from, if you take water from a stream, you need to boil it or put iodine in it, to kill germs and parasites."

"Oh. I see," the cat said thoughtfully. "There is none of that here. You should be able to drink the water without a problem." She licked her paw.

Chad knelt on the grassy bank and refilled his water bottles, drank one, and refilled it again. The water tasted clean and was so cold his teeth ached before he finished drinking the one-liter bottle. "It's good water," he commented as he put the bottles into his pack.

"It is," she replied. "Are we going to sit here all day talking about water, or can we get going?"

"Yeah. I'm up for getting out of here. You lead the way?" Chad asked.

"Yes. Follow me, and stay close. If I suddenly run away, you stay right where you are. You're the biggest thing around here right now, so there's nothing that can hurt you badly. I'm small. It's a little more dangerous for me sometimes."

Chad pulled the black box from his backpack and waved it around. The cat looked at him and shook her head. "I told you. You can put that thing away. It won't work again while I'm around and I'm here to get you through the next gateway."

"Right," Chad said. "I'm just having a little trouble with talking to a cat. The box, I had gotten used to. So, if you could just give me a break, Cat, we can move on."

"Fair enough," the cat said. "My name is Shadow. Though I like being a cat, it's not my name. Come on, we don't have much time. We can talk as we walk."

Shadow seemed to smile, then turned and walked, keeping the line of trees to their left.

Chad shook his head and followed after her. "Shadow," he began when he caught up to her, "I could have sworn you just smiled at me. I hear your voice, or at least 'a voice' I assume is yours, though your lips don't move. Can you tell me how that works?"

"Sure. Come along and I'll try to fill you in."

For some time, they followed the slowly undulating green plain, keeping the oak forest a respectable distance away. The mist-grey sky, consistent and heavy, hung unchanged overhead. For a cat, Shadow walked at a quick, even pace. Chad had always thought of cats as either sitting or running, nothing in between. He was pleasantly surprised to be able to walk at a comfortable speed for some time without a lot of stopping and starting.

As soon as they found a speed that was satisfactory for both of them, Shadow began. "I'm not really a cat. I like this form. It can be fast, it uses energy efficiently, and I know it is one you can understand. The truth is, I don't believe you would even be able to see me as I normally appear. You said I was the first creature you had seen in this world. Have you truly seen no others as you've passed through our dimension?"

"Other creatures?" Chad asked. "No, you're the first I've seen. Are there others?"

He thought the cat was chuckling. "Yes. Of course. There are creatures everywhere. I've just told you there are. But like I said, there is nothing here that can hurt you."

"That's kind of spooky." Chad shivered a bit, "To be surrounded by invisible creatures."

"No, they're not invisible, only imperceptible to your mind. If you were to stay in our dimension for a time, you would begin to see the others more plainly. I am projecting this image to your mind so you may perceive my presence. I project my voice as well as my emotions so you may better understand my words."

They walked for only a short time before Chad asked another question.

"How did you know I was coming?" he asked with a quick glance down at the cat.

Shadow spoke in her typical casual tone. "We didn't, until just last night. We recognized the Star Daughter when she was brought through the gate. We knew, or rather, hoped you would be soon after her. If the gate had closed before you could come through, your chances of catching up to her would have been greatly reduced."

"Okay. Now I have about a thousand more questions." Chad shook his head, exasperated at the number of new ideas the cat had just proposed. "First, you said 'we' a couple of times. Who is we?" Chad stumbled over the awkward grammar.

"This is a transitional dimension. You could even call it a buffer between the prime dimension, which is the Earth where you reside, and the deeper, more malleable dimensions to come. In the buffer dimensions agents of the Starside and the Cloudside are present. Almost an equilibrium. It's why we allowed you to be guided by the box for so long. The Cloudside will have less claim on you now. Their turn was over, and their influence on you will be weak for some time."

"I need to know right off if this is magic. I'm really not comfortable with magic, so I would like that to be clear," Chad said with what he felt was righteous assertiveness.

"No," Shadow said. "Magic is a power unknown to us and would alter the laws of science to bring a result that is otherwise impossible. There is no unknown power here. What we are discussing is more of a technology used to bend energy within the laws of physics."

Shadow paused and looked up at Chad as they walked. "You look to be in your early adolescence. Is that correct?"

"Yes," Chad agreed.

"Then I will assume you don't have any advanced understanding of physics, and won't try to explain the intricacies of these dimensions. There is no magic. There are dimensions that are malleable, plastic, and moldable. Some are more easily moldable than others. Those are the most desirable dimensions. And the battle for control of these prime locations is escalating, as you obviously must be aware as you are in pursuit of the Star Daughter and her captor."

"No. I am most definitely not aware of any battle for control. And you keep mentioning stars and Star Daughters. I didn't see any stars during the night."

"Look up at the sky. What do you see?" the cat asked.

"I don't see anything," he mumbled thoughtfully as he looked up. "Maybe fog? Or clouds, I guess."

"Clouds. Of course." He heard her voice drop behind him and looked back to see she had stopped walking. When he walked back to her, she stared ahead blankly and Chad could hear her humming. There was no true melody, nor repeating chorus. It sounded more like she was humming scales, and then arpeggios. At times Chad thought she may have even hummed a chord.

She stopped and looked up at Chad. "Look now," she said. "What do you see?"

Chad looked back at the sky. Through the haze of fog, he could see several faint pinpricks of light, like the shooting stars you see when you stand up suddenly and your head spins. These were stationary though, and were easier to see if not looked at directly.

"Yeah," Chad said. "I can see a few stars. And in the daytime, too. How'd you do that? I thought you said you didn't do magic."

"It's not magic, Chad. And I'm getting tired of repeating myself," Shadow said though she was smiling again. "I just projected sounds you could hear. Sound is waves of energy. Energy can be used to unlock or activate different technologies. Different sized waves make different sounds. Music is a combination of sounds, of waves. It's a technology. In fact, it was the technology that opened up the dimensions for travel a thousand years ago."

Shadow started walking again and Chad followed along behind. At times he glanced up at the newfound stars, at times he thought about the idea of music being technology. Ultimately his thoughts returned to stars.

"So, who's on the Starside, and who is the Star Daughter?" he asked when he remembered he had wanted to know about the stars.

"Think about it, Chad. Who do you think the Star Daughter would be?"

"Amy?" he guessed.

"That's right. And those on the Starside would be anyone who's aligned with her, to help her achieve her purpose. And before you ask, we don't know what her purpose is. She probably doesn't know either, only that she has a responsibility to carry out in the dimensions which will bring about a major change. Possibly alter the structure of the human societies as they have functioned for the past thousand years.

"What the Cloudside knows, and what they have in other dimensions, I don't know. This is what we have, and I mean those of us on the Starside in this transitional zone. Some would call this a prophecy; others would call it reading the harmonic waves. It translates like this in your language:

When the storm comes and the clouds gather, the winds will blow the stars from the sky.
The dark wind brings the Star Daughter from obscurity into obscurity, while her Champion follows in the calm.
Together they will break the ground, and from obscurity return light to a new sky.

Shadow stopped walking and looked directly into Chad's eyes. "If you don't know who the Star Daughter's Champion is, it's time for you to go back to the trail and head into the oak forest. Because, if you're too dim to figure that one out, I think she would be better off without your help."

10 - What's in a Name

"No, I guess I'm not that dense," Chad said, feeling a little overwhelmed. "If the Star Daughter is Amy and she is followed by her Champion, it must be me. Mr. Snider told me that since I was the one who made it possible for Derrick to take her away, I must be the one to bring her back. From your poem, or prophecy, it sounds like they have her buried somewhere."

"Yes," Shadow said. "It is likely they will take her to the deepest dimension they are able. But they can only take her so deep. To take someone through a gate against their will requires energy. The stronger the Cloudside influence on the dimension, the more energy it will require to get Amy through. Since she is the Star Daughter, I would say the most they will be able to get her through before their available energy is spent is three, maybe four gates."

Chad thought about that. "You don't think they might try to hide her on a Starside dimension or one more neutral?"

"No. The more time they spend in a dimension with a Starside majority, the greater their risk of detection. Just like clouds block light in the sky and light shines in darkness. The stronger your alignment to one side or the other, the more apparent your alignment will be to others. My guess is they will try to win her over to their side, or at least try to get her to sympathize. That will make her less visible to those trying to find her."

Chad shook himself in frustration. "There's so much I have to think about here. This is a transitional dimension from my world, right, Shadow?"

The cat nodded.

"So, does everyone who enters the dimensions come through this one, and do they have as much trouble grasping things as I do?"

"No," Shadow replied. "There are several of these buffer dimensions, though they are few compared to the total number of discovered dimensions. Each of the buffers has an equilibrium of the Cloudside or Starside.

Each side has attempted to gain a majority in the buffers, though it has never been achieved."

She paused a moment before she continued, "And don't feel bad. You're actually doing pretty well for someone who wasn't raised in the dimensions."

Chad gave up on asking questions which seemed to only bring on more confusion. Instead, he pondered all Shadow had said while they silently climbed and descended each of the low rolling hills.

Shadow eventually continued, "There is only one entrance from the prime dimension into a buffer at any time—occasionally there is no entrance at all. There are typically two or three exits, and yes, before you ask, we are headed to the exit they took the Star Daughter through. I only hope we can get there before it closes."

"Mr. Snider told me I would need keys to get through the portals," Chad said. "The game player was the key that got me into this dimension. What key do we have to get through this next one?"

"*I* am the key to the next portal," Shadow said, puffing herself up importantly. "When a person, or persons, cast a portal, they, or any piece of their personal property can be used as a key. Derrick, probably with a good amount of help, cast that portal you came through, which is why his game player worked to get you through."

"For naturally forming portals like the one we will use to exit, any resident of that dimension becomes a key and can assist you through from either side. Also, that box you have is Cloudside technology and will get you through most portals having a Cloudside alignment.

"Will you be going through to the next dimension with me?" he asked, trying not to sound as nervous as he was.

"Yes and no. I will take you through the portal, though I cannot stay. I am a creature of the buffer dimension." Chad was mildly surprised to hear sympathy in her voice. "I have never left this dimension before and can't stay out of it long."

"How will I know where to go once I've crossed to the next dimension?" Chad asked, feeling slightly bewildered.

"How did you know where to go in this dimension?"

"I didn't," Chad said, annoyed. "I got here and started wandering, following the box."

"Seems to have worked for you pretty well so far," the cat remarked. "It looks like you might have an aptitude for this kind of thing. But, as I said earlier, those with the strongest alignment are easiest to recognize. If you can find someone aligned with your cause, they may be able to travel through gates and guide you better. Stay alert as you make your way deeper. There will be more gates in and out of those dimensions."

Shadow stopped so abruptly Chad nearly stepped on her. She looked from side to side rapidly and suddenly ran for the tree line. She shouted back to Chad as she ran, "Wait there."

The cat was gone in an instant, disappearing into the ancient oaks. Their huge, gnarled branches twisted and intertwined like the muscled arms of wrestling giants, creating a thick, protective ceiling above the floor of the woods.

Chad looked around himself nervously and wondered what had frightened the cat so much she would run away so suddenly. What unseen creatures were likely to be milling about at his feet? Sure, Shadow had told him none were big enough to do him harm. But still, could they bite his legs? Or inject venom? Even insects could kill a man under the right circumstances. And what about snakes? He remembered how he had sat in the grass earlier, and on the trail. What manner of creatures crawled around him at those times?

Panic crept up the back of Chad's neck, making the small hairs stand up. Sweat broke out across his back and trickled down his spine. He wanted to run to a safe place, but where would he go?

The next moment, Shadow was back.

"Whoa. You're back," Chad said and was quickly embarrassed he had stated something so obvious. Trying to recover his composure, he asked, "Have they left already?"

Starting off down the trail again, Shadow asked, "Have who left?"

"I don't know, who- or whatever it was that chased you up that tree." As he spoke, he found he was getting used to feeling confused. He had felt this way much of the time since he had met Shadow.

"Oh," Shadow said. She never broke stride, but maintained a dedicated course along the oak forest. "I'm sorry," she continued eventually. "Nothing chased me up the tree. I just wanted to check our course and progress. We're close to the next portal. We should be there before nightfall.

"Well, that's comforting," he said, feeling anything but comforted.

Either Shadow missed the sarcasm in his voice or else she chose not to respond to it. She continued to walk ahead of him for some time before speaking again. Without preamble, she asked, "What's your family name, Chad?"

"Baker," he replied simply.

"No. Not their occupation. What is the family name? The fact you are walking the dimensions and jumping portals, shows you have blood of one of the old families. The families who have lived in these dimensions for a thousand years."

"Oh, right. Mrs. Walker did mention a name," he said thoughtfully, and asked himself, "Now, what was it? Oh, yeah. Lorantelle."

He was just congratulating himself for remembering the name, when he realized Shadow was gone again. She hadn't run off—there was nowhere she could go and hide that quickly. Then, like a character in a science fiction movie, she flickered back into view, at times in the form of a cat, at times as what appeared to be a headless tortoise covered in brambles and thorns. The images flipped back and forth so rapidly, they appeared together simultaneously, as a gray cat wearing a green-and-brown camouflaged tortoise shell.

Suddenly, she was back and appeared as solid and catlike as when they had first met. Licking at her shoulder three or four times, she headed back down the trail. "We need to hurry. It's getting close to dusk, and we really should get you through the portal before then."

Chad was still astounded and confused by the unusual display he had just witnessed. When he finally found his voice, he asked, "Are you going to tell me what just happened? That was the weirdest thing I have ever seen, and now you're acting like it was nothing unusual."

"Happened?" asked the cat. "Oh, that. You startled me and I couldn't hold onto my assumed shape. As you can see now, I have regained control of my emotions."

"I startled you?" Chad asked, amazed.

"Yes, I didn't expect you to tell me you're a Lorantelle. In fact, if I were you, I would hesitate to mention that name to almost anyone you meet in these dimensions. It is not a very good name to have."

"It's not? The Sniders told me it was a pretty good name."

"Perhaps it was at one time," she conceded. "But right now, unless you're ready for a fight or just don't want to have anyone else help you, you might want to keep that information to yourself."

Before Chad could form a reply, Shadow spoke again. "Here's the portal. You haven't much time to get through before it fades. Once it's gone, it could take hours to find the new gateway. Get going."

At the edge of the oak wood, incongruous to the trees to its sides, stood a pitch-black doorway large enough to drive a full-sized pickup through. Light shimmered off its obsidian surface.

Chad didn't hesitate, just charged toward the liquid black portal, the cat close on his heels. Together, they stepped through to the next dimension.

"Thanks, Shadow," he said as he turned and looked back at the shimmering wall. "I hope we meet again. I've enjoyed our talk, and I still have a lot of questions."

"Good luck, Chad. And good journey. Much depends on your success," Shadow said as she jumped back through.

Chad waved lamely at the cat through the portal and watched the gateway fade just moments later.

The cat's voice came to him faintly, "Lorantelle used to be a strong name—a good name. Maybe it will be again."

11 - A New Neighborhood

Chad turned in circles a few times and looked around.

"Yup. It's gone," he said, "But, what did I expect?"

He felt alone again—even more so than after entering the transitional dimension. Shadow had become his first friend in the dimensions and he missed having her around already.

He stood in a field. The dark green grass reached nearly to his calves. Around the large, empty, square lot were the back fences of houses—some made of tall, wide boards, some of narrow grape-stake, while some were merely metal cyclone fencing that allowed passersby to see right into their yards.

"This could be my neighborhood," he said as he looked at the fences and the houses beyond.

The sun appeared to be heading toward sunset. That would follow if the dimensions were all in the same time zone.

Shadow had said there would be more gates in and out of these inner dimensions. Chad needed to find Amy before she was moved too far for him to locate, yet he had absolutely no idea which direction to go.

The box. He hated to rely on that thing again, but what options did he have? Shadow said there would be Cloudside influence in this dimension to some extent, and if he used the box he might alert the Cloudside he was here. For now, he chose to walk.

He wandered along the concrete sidewalk of a suburban street. With white stucco walls and large, multi-paned windows and wood shingled roofs, the houses sat amid manicured lawns and neatly tended flower beds. Stately trees stood tall above the sidewalks and drives.

"Well, the houses are too big and old for my neighborhood. This looks more like Amy's." He thought of the ancient oaks and maples in Amy's yard and wondered if they'd been transplanted from this dimension.

He walked a good distance down one street, looking for a street name, a mail box, or some other indicator of who lived in the houses. At an intersection of two broad streets it occurred to him, he hadn't seen a single car, person, or other creature since coming through the portal.

"Or, maybe they're all around me, but I just can't see them." The idea made him shiver.

Chad sat on the curb. His stomach rumbled and he considered eating one of the packages of ramen noodles, dry. He often did as a snack at home. Instead, he drank some water.

Reaching again into his backpack, he took out the black box. He hoped to see a red indicator light as in the past, but was disappointed. He pressed the circular power switch with his thumb. Nothing happened. He had seen both Derek and Mrs. Walker operate the box, but couldn't get it to do anything for himself. Turning it over, he checked to see if there were any instructions written on the back he may have missed, but was disappointed again.

Frustrated by his lack of progress, he said aloud, "How on earth am I going to find Amy?"

The screen of the game player flashed to life. The high definition display revealed an image of Amy's face with such detail and clarity, Chad could easily believe she had been shrunk and trapped inside the box.

He looked closely at the image and saw she was speaking rapidly. At times, her eyes narrowed with anger. She looked pale and sweaty, and her hair hung around her face in dirty tangles. Chad brought the game player close to his face to see if he could find any clues to where she might be. As he did, his thumb brushed one side of the device and Amy's image spun until Chad was looking at the back of her head. He tried to look past her to see who she was speaking to, but only saw blackness around her.

He brushed his thumb along the device's side once more and sent Amy's head spinning around again. By repeating the gesture he was able to keep her head spinning like a top, and her features blurred into horizontal lines.

He laughed. "Mrs. Walker never mentioned anything like this."

Instantly, Amy's image vanished, and the wrinkled, angry visage of his formidable English teacher appeared in its place, her eyes half closed. At first, Chad thought her image was a static photograph, but soon saw her mouth some words, like she was absorbed in reading.

Understanding hit him. "My mother," he spoke to the screen.

Immediately the view changed to his mother's face. It shifted about as if she was involved in an activity—cleaning, shopping, working, etc. Chad carefully set the device on the sidewalk and pulled the cellphone from his backpack, then powered it on. Still fully charged. He sent a text to his mother.

Mom, I crossed to the next dimension. Tell Mr. Snider it looks like home, but no people yet.

He sent the text and waited a moment. As he expected, the expression on his mother's face registered surprise at what must have been her phone alerting her to the incoming message.

Chad watched her face change from pleasure to understanding, then concern, and at last to resolve as she read the message. She held the phone to her ear as she spoke with someone.

Chad quickly said, "Mr. Snider," and expected to see Amy's father with a phone to his ear as well. Instead Mr. Snider's head bobbed and swayed as if he was walking quickly or climbing a steep path.

"Oh. Mrs. Snider," Chad exclaimed, and her head appeared, a phone held to ear.

"Mother," he said again. He watched her speak for some time, gratified she at least had found some companionship in Amy's mother.

He began to put the device away, but on an impulse said, "Derrick."

The screen went blank.

"Hmm," Chad considered. "Maybe that's not his real name."

He got back to his feet and looked around. It was late afternoon and the sun was descending toward evening. A light came on in the house behind him.

"That's a good sign," Chad said.

He walked to the front door and knocked.

He waited a minute, then pushed the doorbell. It sounded just like home. He felt like he could be standing at the door of any number of kids he knew, and not in another dimension with good and evil sides competing for power.

When no one answered, he knocked again, not knowing what else to do. He was not in the habit of walking into people's homes uninvited, but he was getting desperate. He tried the door handle. It gave way smoothly and the door slipped open a few inches.

"Hello?" he called into the house. There was no reply. He pushed the door open further and stepped into the entryway.

"Hello?" he said again, but without truly expecting an answer. He thought again of the invisible creatures of the previous dimension and reasoned if there had been any in this home, they surely would have heard the door bell and would not be surprised to find him wandering through their home.

He closed the door and walked into the tidy, neatly furnished front room. To the right it opened into a dining room and kitchen beyond. The hallway directly ahead of him must lead to bedrooms and hopefully a bathroom. He crossed to the hallway and found the hoped-for bathroom beyond the first door on the left. Before entering, he said, "If anyone can hear me, I'm sorry to intrude on your privacy. I just need to use your bathroom."

He entered the small room, locked the door behind himself, and looked carefully around. There were fresh pink towels hanging from a rack on the wall, a bar of glycerin soap in a glass dish next to the sink, and a whole roll of toilet paper waiting patiently in a dispenser on the wall.

Having taken care of business he stepped into the hallway and considered the extra roll of toilet paper under a crocheted cover at the back of the toilet. It would really come in handy if he couldn't find another house when the need arose again, but he felt wrong stealing anything more than hospitality and left it behind.

Though it felt like he was in there for a short time, the house had darkened considerably while he was in the bathroom. Flipping off the light in the small room left the rest of the house in shadows as Chad carefully worked his way across the sitting room and felt for the handle on the front door.

His mind on where to go and what to do next, he swung the front door open.

With a shout of surprise, he fell back and landed so hard it knocked the breath from him. Gasping for air, he struggled to back away from the open doorway.

Silhouetted against the gray twilight was a creature, maned like a lion with clawed hands outstretched. It leapt at him where he sat on the floor, wheezing and spluttering. Chad was pinned beneath its weight as it reached down and took hold of both his shoulders with its taloned grip.

"Are you alright?" The voice was soft and gentle, a girl's voice or a woman's, with the hint of an unfamiliar accent. She left his side, turned on a table lamp, and returned to kneel by his shoulder.

"I'm sorry," Chad said, finally finding enough air to fill his lungs. "In the doorway you looked like... Well, I was surprised."

Chad found it difficult to speak coherently to the beautiful girl who leaned over him. She looked to be in her late teens and had a mane of auburn red hair that would be the envy of any fashion model. That hair shimmered in the incandescent glow of the table lamp.

"Oh," Chad began again. "I'm sorry I'm in your house. I just had to, well, you know, use the john."

Chad felt heat on his cheeks and forehead as he blushed. The girl's brown eyes sparkled as she smiled at him.

"Don't worry. Here, let me help you up," she said and stood, offering her hand to Chad. Her fingers were slender and delicate with long, manicured nails painted blood red. She wore a loose white cotton blouse with a crocheted flower pattern at the neck and wrist. Her jeans were naturally faded to a light blue.

Chad reached up and took her hands, then gasped and tried to pull back when a static electric shock snapped between their fingertips as they touched. Strangely, the shock didn't end in an instant as he expected, but diminished in intensity and remained as a faint vibration between their hands as long as they were in contact. He looked at the girl and saw she had a similar look of surprise on her face.

Getting to his feet, he rubbed his hands together until the strange sensation faded, then rubbed his backside where he had landed.

The girl winked. "I'm Amanda. What's your name?" She smiled at him, flipped her hair out of her face with an endearing twitch, and extended her hand again, this time in greeting.

He tentatively grasped her fingers and was only slightly less surprised at the sudden shock and residual buzzing in the muscles of his hand and forearm as she squeezed gently.

"I'm Chad," he said, confusion apparent in his voice. "What is with the shock you keep giving me?"

She smiled again and shook her head. He almost wished she would stop smiling. His heart jumped each time she did that, and he didn't know how much of it he could take before his heart stopped altogether.

She frowned a little at his question, which Chad also found attractive. "I'm not sure why, myself. But I think it may have something to do with the Star Daughter."

She appeared uncertain for the first time since they had met. "You are her Champion, aren't you?"

Chad hesitated a moment. "I don't mean to sound suspicious, or mistrusting. You've been kind to me so far, but what do you know about the Star Daughter and her Champion? And how am I to know whose side you are on?"

She frowned again. She had a perfect mouth with naturally red lips and dimples that persisted through her changing expressions. Eventually she conceded and said, "I'm not sure how to make you trust me, or know we are on the same side. Regardless, Amy's my cousin and I'm here to help you."

12 - Friends and Enemies

"Commander Lorantelle," a voice spoke softly from behind him, nearly lost in the open air outside the Chateau. "His highness wishes to speak with you."

The commander remained with his back to the messenger as he looked out over a lush green valley. Hands flat on the low stone wall, he barely kept his fury in check. "His highness, is it? Well then, let *his highness* know I will be in presently."

"Yes, sir," the messenger said hesitantly. Lorantelle heard a light scuffing on the gravel path as the aide backed away then turned and strode off.

Giving the boy enough time to be fully away, Lorantelle took a deep breath to steady himself and faced the villa, headquarters of the Dimensional Resistance. It was an impressive structure, built during the French Renaissance, and echoed the prevailing architecture during that era in the Prime Earth Dimension. He crossed a broad terracotta patio and climbed polished marble steps to the villa. "His highness," he muttered as he mounted the stair.

During his time in the dimensions, Lorantelle had only been to the villa on two occasions, both outdoor banquets. He had never been within the walls of "his highness's" command center and residence. To have been summoned here this day filled the commander with ominous foreboding.

Once through the heavily inlaid oak doors all, semblance of the French villa disappeared.

The large rectangular entry had the appearance of a modern office suite: glass and chrome furniture, black and gray granite floor tiles, and computer work stations. A bank of HD video screens stretched the length of one wall, showcasing scenes from the perimeter of the villa and of many of the rooms within.

Just through the door, access to the rest of the chamber was blocked by an unadorned glass table where a woman sat, straight and imposing, her hands folded in her lap. Young and slender, with long, wavy chestnut hair, the receptionist would have been beautiful if not for the permanent scowl that creased her brow and narrowed her eyes. An attractive ruffled peach blouse and straight black knee length skirt, visible through the table, accentuated her figure but did little to soften her overall appearance of contempt.

The commander stopped near the desk and said with as little emotion and inflection as possible, "His Eminence has summoned me."

Though it seemed impossible, the woman's scowl deepened. "Indeed," she said and placed her hands flat on the tabletop. Green florescent light flashed from the chrome border and showed through the glass. She swept her hand across one area and touched a fingertip to the table's glowing surface in another. A door behind her slipped silently open. She returned her glare to Lorantelle. "You may enter."

He followed a long, sterile passage lit by florescent panels recessed into the plastered ceiling. He noticed the occasional unmarked door as he passed through the estate to the far end of the building. The door was already ajar as he approached the reclusive leader's chambers.

"Commander, come in," he heard as he raised his hand to knock.

The decor inside the office was a return to the French renaissance. Antique furniture and lush carpets decorated the room and paintings by "The Masters" adorned the dark wood-paneled walls.

Lorantelle stepped to the middle of the room, went to one knee, bowed his head, and gave the expected address. "My lord, I am here."

A man sat behind the desk, his jet-black hair plastic in its perfection. The unlined face gave him the appearance of a much younger man. No one knew how old Lord Caltone was, exactly, though many who were much older than Lorantelle's forty-two years had served the enigmatic leader for their entire lives.

"You may rise, Commander Lorantelle," Lord Caltone said. Without waiting for Lorantelle to do so, he continued, "I have a task for you."

Lorantelle stood as casually as possible and concentrated on maintaining a blank expression while he waited for the ruler to continue.

A light breeze shifted the lace curtains in the large open window. Lord Caltone looked out the window at the rolling hills below and took several long breaths before speaking again. "An intruder has entered our lands. I want you to eliminate him."

Lorantelle followed the leader's gaze as he continued to stare out the window. "I assume you refer to the Star Daughter's Champion. Is the girl here, in the Villa?"

Caltone turned back to Lorantelle with a jerk of his head, and scowled. He half-stood and leaned forward onto the desk. He narrowed his eyes at the commander and settled back into the leather upholstered wooden chair. His gaze cut through the commander as he regained his composure, and said, woodenly, "Our mutual enmity doesn't justify such insubordination, Commander Lorantelle. If there is something I wish you to know, I will share it with you."

The commander felt his anger rising, having grown tired of "his highness's" games.

"Well, my lord," Lorantelle said and folded his arms across his chest. "If you want me to stop this intruder, and he is looking for the Star Daughter, it would make sense to start from the intruder's destination and work outward. However, if you wish me to strike out blindly through the dimensions, I can do that, too. If this constitutes insubordination, well..."

Lorantelle let his words hang like bait before a shark.

The only outward sign of Caltone's displeasure was a slight twitch in his left eye. At last he spoke. "Commander Lorantelle, your attitude displeases me. Your lack of participation in our efforts over the last few years has been regrettable and frustrating to say the least. I had hoped you would see this mission as an opportunity to reestablish yourself as a leader in our cause. If you wish to remove yourself from this campaign, I am certain we can find an appropriate, out-of-the-way place for you to reside."

"My lord," Lorantelle said and lowered his head slightly as a sign of respect. He wanted to appease the powerful man but also feared backing down too much would make him appear weak. After a moment, he continued, "I don't understand why you feel the need to threaten me, or attempt to manipulate me into this assignment. I intended no insult, nor meant to imply I was unwilling to take on this task. I willingly accept and if you wish me to cast about the countryside without direction then let me begin immediately."

Lorantelle wheeled and marched toward the door.

"I have the girl," Caltone said abruptly as Lorantelle reached for the polished brass handle.

Lorantelle froze where he was, then turned slowly, his fist still gripping the handle. Caltone repeated, "I have the girl, the Star Daughter. She was brought in yesterday. She is safely below, in the wine cellar."

Grey eyes met the icy blue of Caltone's and locked.

"Yes, commander," Caltone said. "You may speak with her, if you must. Indeed, if you can get anything out of her, I would even be indebted to you for your efforts. Speak with Julia at the front desk. She will call an escort to take you to the cellars. You're dismissed."

Caltone turned his attention to the glass sheet that covered the wooden desktop and shifted his hands across its surface.

"What's your name, boy?" Lorantelle asked his escort—the same messenger who had initially invited him into the villa—as they descended countless steps into the wine cellar.

"My name is Felipe Constantia," the boy said. He sounded almost cheery to have been asked such a personal question.

"How old are you, Felipe, and have you worked here long?" Lorantelle continued his friendly interrogation.

"I am sixteen years old, and I don't know if I should be answering any questions about the villa," the boy said nervously. "Lord Cal— or rather, his highness discourages discussion of the villa or its grounds."

"Don't worry, Felipe," Lorantelle said in a comforting manner, "I wouldn't think of risking your position or employment with his highness.

Their shadows played leapfrog as they passed periodic lights set in the wall of the circular stairwell.

On the lowest floor, Lorantelle and his guide entered the main cellar through a heavy wooden door and passed row after dusty row of wine bottles in wooden racks. They found the girl at the end of the aisle, between the brick wall and the last rack of wine bottles.

"Here she is," Felipe said.

"I see that," Lorantelle said dryly, and turned toward her in the shadows.

She sat on a plain wooden chair. Her hands were bound with duct tape and then secured to the chair back behind her. Her legs were taped to the legs of the chair as well. Her hair hung down around her face in dirty tangles, and her face was sweaty and smeared with dirt and grime.

Lorantelle was surprised to find there were no tear tracks running through the dust and smudges on her face.

"Felipe." Lorantelle did his best to sound incensed as he shouted at the boy who stood at his back. "How can you treat this girl so poorly? She may be the enemy, but she is still a guest."

Lorantelle's sudden reprimand caught Felipe off guard and he looked stunned and embarrassed. "Commander," he defended, "we allow her to get up every two hours to walk around and to, well, walk around. But she is a prisoner, after all."

"I'm sorry they're treating you so poorly, young lady," Lorantelle said in an attempt to sound compassionate. "I'll see to it your conditions here improve." He took a folding knife from his pocket and slit the bands holding her hands and arms.

She rubbed her numb wrists, held her head high, and her back straight. If hate were a blade, her eyes would have sliced him in two. She glared at him and said nothing.

"What is your name, girl?" he asked more abruptly.

Still she sat in defiant silence.

"Who are your parents?" he tried again. "I can let them know you're okay."

She only glared harder.

He knelt in front of her and said, "Look. I want to help you, but you need to give me something to work with."

"You want to help me?" Her eyes were brilliant flames. "Let me out of here and I'll get my own help. I don't need any from someone like you."

"I'm sorry, I can't let you out," he said sympathetically. He stood and turned his back to her to hide his smile. He had her now. She had spoken. It would be simple to bend her to his will.

13 - Power, for what it's Worth.

Lorantelle stood in the shadows. The girl had clammed up immediately after Derrick began his interrogation hours before, and he didn't want his presence to interfere with the information the boy was gleaning.

Derrick had a nasty, cynical attitude and used tone of voice and body position to intimidate the girl into speaking. This kid was a natural bully. He teased and tempted, coerced and cajoled, until Amy burst out in anger, opening flood gates of emotion, information, and most importantly, vocal patterns Lorantelle could lock onto and use to his advantage.

"Come on, Amy," Derrick sneered. "We know Snider's not your real name. What is that, German? There have never been any Sniders in the dimensions, and no names here even sound like that. Tell us who you are, who you really are, and we can help you."

"Help me?" Amy asked. Her words bounced off the brick walls of the wine cellar as her voice rose in pitch and volume. "Help me do what?"

Lorantelle listened intently to find the pattern or rhythm to her speech. It usually required only a phrase or two to lock onto something he could manipulate to his advantage. But something in this girl's words prevented him from holding onto them. He scratched his short salt and pepper hair and turned his attention back to the interrogation.

Derrick stepped back theatrically as if Amy had physically slapped him. He shook his head. A dazed and silly grin of astonishment spread across his face, and he said, "Help us unite our people, Star Daughter."

The boy walked far enough behind Amy that she wasn't able to see him no matter how she craned her neck. He leaned against a dusty wooden wine rack and crossed his arms over his chest. The smile was gone from his face and in the dimness of the cellar his squinting eyes almost glowed with intensity. In a voice so low it was unclear if he spoke to himself or to the girl,

Derrick continued, "We know the prophecy, just like you do. You know that's why you're here."

Amy gave up straining to see the boy behind her. Relaxing her neck she stared at the rough stone floor in front of her, her head bowed and tilted slightly to the side. She looked forlorn and beaten. Lorantelle had a sudden and uncharacteristic pang of sympathy as he thought of how his parents must have broken under interrogation. He quickly reminded himself of his responsibilities. She might be young and vulnerable, unlike the powerful and dangerous masters of her class, yet this girl was still the enemy. If the prophecy had any validity, she was a pivotal piece in the coming dimensional changes. If her skills could be turned to the Cloudside's purposes, there would be no stopping Caltone and his followers.

When she spoke again, Amy's voice was even quieter and more distant than Derrick's had been. "I don't know anything about a prophecy and the only reason I'm here is because you tricked my friend into giving me to you."

"Friend?" Lorantelle blurted from the shadows.

Amy looked up from the floor, toward the sound of his voice. Angry with himself for reminding the girl he was there, his irritation flared when Derrick scowled and stepped forward to continue his interrogation. Derrick must have known who had put the girl in his hands, yet he had not shared that information with Lorantelle. They were wasting time with the girl when it was obvious who her Champion was. Her "friend" must be found and eliminated.

"So many lies, Amy." Derrick leaned forward, his face close to hers. "Isn't that just like your people? You're always mixing in a little truth with the lies to make your deception credible."

Amy said nothing, but glared at the boy who gloated under the single bare light bulb glowing weakly in the narrow corridor of the wine cellar. She winced as Derrick forced a sudden, barking laugh and said, "Your people have been in control of the dimensions for a thousand years now. You can't maintain that hold in these modern times. Your leaders can no longer disregard the desires and the rights of the people—of all the people."

"The rights of the people?" Amy spat the words with such vehemence Derrick backed up a half a step, though he maintained his condescending sneer. "It's your people, not mine, that have perpetrated campaigns of misinformation and historical inaccuracies to bolster your tenuous house of cards."

Derrick wiped his face with the back of his sleeve. He turned to leave, looked into the shadows where he knew Lorantelle stood, and winked at the commander. He said over his shoulder to the girl tied to the chair, "Join us, Amy. You can change us. You know that's why you're here."

#

Lorantelle allowed Derrick to walk ahead of him when they exited the cellar.

Felipe waited outside the door with a cup of water, bread, and a few slices of cheese. Derrick took a slice of the cheese as he walked past the other boy, who scowled and pulled the tray away, though at that point, it was a useless gesture.

Derrick shoved the cheese in his mouth, headed up the circular stairs, and laughed. "Went well, don't you think?"

Catching him on the stairway leading up to the main floor of the villa, Lorantelle grasped the boy's shoulder and spun him around. "No, I don't think it went so well."

Derrick's mouth fell open in shock. Bits of cheese clung to his teeth and lips, until his surprise turned slowly to anger. "What do you mean? I had her spilling her guts in there."

"'Spilling her guts?' She hardly told us anything. In fact, the only thing of import we learned in there is you that already know who the Champion is." Lorantelle's own indignation gave fire to his words. "And you have known since the moment you secured the girl for us."

Derrick said nothing, his face a mask of conceit and hate.

"You're as stupid as you are arrogant." Lorantelle pushed past the boy and leapt up the stairs. "Don't just stand there like the simpleton you are," he called from the top. "I need the information you have locked in your thick skull, and I'm tired of standing around in the dark."

#

Lorantelle strode directly toward Julia at her glass and chrome desk. Derrick followed sullenly, several steps behind.

"We need a conference room with data pads, access to the Family Genetic Data Base, and something to eat," Lorantelle snapped at the secretary.

He didn't think the woman could have sat any straighter in her seat or worn a more severe expression on her face. However, when Lorantelle spoke, Julia became the personification of a marble pillar. She turned stiffly to him, her brows arched and her eyes narrowed. "Commander Lorantelle. I am sure you are aware how late it is. It is quite impossible to accommodate such requests without sufficient advance notice."

Incensed, he took the final step to the glass table, leaned across it, and poked his index finger an inch from

133

the secretary's nose. "I'm sick of insolent, ineffectual subordinates like you and your boy over here, with your self-serving and obstructive requirements. You're delaying me and putting our entire mission at risk."

Lorantelle took a quick breath, closed his eyes, and said, much more calmly than he felt, "You'll get me a conference room, now, and send Felipe in with some food, now, or you, me, and Henry Kissinger over there will march down the passage to Lord Caltone's office and have a picnic on his very expensive throw rugs."

Julia's face drained of all color and then flared back to a fiery red as a voice spoke from the intercom embedded in the glass table top. "Julia. Do as he asks."

"Yes, Lord Caltone." She passed her hand across the glass desk. Fluorescent greens and purples flashed from the chrome edges. Julia tapped here and there on the desktop and then looked up at the commander.

Palm up, she indicated a door off the main lobby. "You may use this conference room," she said. "There are data pads as you have requested. Felipe will be in with some bread and cheese, as it is well past the evening meal."

Lorantelle and Derrick turned in the indicated direction as the door swung open, inviting them in.

#

Lorantelle placed a small piece of the brown bread smeared with soft cheese into his mouth and chewed while across from him Derrick stuffed bite after bite of bread and cheese into his mouth. Lorantelle shook his head, marveling at how quickly his attitudes and opinions had changed lately. This morning, he would have considered it absurd to take an active part in this—what was it? Revolution? Succession? Overthrow?

And the boy Derrick? At first, the commander considered him a gifted tactician, a ruthless interrogator, a prodigy. Now, Lorantelle could see he was no different than any other petulant, self-absorbed teenager.

"Who was the friend the girl spoke of when you questioned her?" Lorantelle asked the boy who appeared to have finally reached his capacity for food.

"Friend?" Derrick asked, stupidly.

"Oh, for the sake of the dimensions," Lorantelle cried, grasping fists of his hair. Jumping to his feet he leaned across the small table brought in for their late dinner. "The friend. The one who sold out our little captive in the cellars. You do know who she is, don't you?" He gritted his teeth as he spoke, fighting back the urge to shake the boy until the answers tumbled out of him. "You ventured all the way to the prime dimension to find the girl and bring her back here, and you don't know who she is, or who will be following her?"

Derrick got to his feet as well. He stood nose to nose with the commander and set his own jaw to respond. "Of course I know who she is. She's the Star Daughter, supposedly here to unite or divide the peoples of the dimensions." He laughed like the entire story was nonsense. "But she's just some little girl. She doesn't look all that powerful or dangerous to me, tied to that chair between the wine racks."

"You just don't see it, do you?" Lorantelle scowled at the youth who only shrugged. The commander shook his head and ground one fist back and forth into the palm of the other hand. "Let me enhance your perspective. With a single word from her, you, I, even Lord Caltone would be compelled to do what she demands. And there is no way to disobey her command."

With a deep breath, Lorantelle sat back down in the padded armchair. He deserved a medal for his restraint in not throttling Derrick where he stood. The boy was an imbecile. The commander held his hands in front of him as if holding a large invisible ball. "I'll try to make this simple. The Star Daughter is potentially the most powerful person to enter the dimensions, and you simply waltzed up and tricked some kid into giving her to you? Some powerless primer kid?"

"Yeah. Why not? What's the big deal?" Derrick shrugged, still looking belligerent.

"First," the commander said, "to hand over the Star Daughter, your power must be equal to hers. And second, you have to be one of two people: a family member or her Champion. Was the friend a family member?"

"No. Well, I don't think he was related. No one ever said he was. I think he just has a crush on her." Derrick giggled.

"Then he is the Champion, and rather than eliminating him with a single preemptive stroke, you have allowed him to follow you into the dimensions and attempt to rescue her." Derrick's stupidity was beginning to wear on Lorantelle, making it harder to rein in his temper. "Think about it, you foolish child. That little girl down in the cellar has the power to control the dimensions or tear them apart. Now, somewhere in our dimension another of equal power is on his way to rescue her. If the two unite, it won't matter how many we persuade to our side. We can only lose.

"He was just some kid," Derrick whined, worry finally breaking through his bravado.

"We can only hope he believes the same about himself," Commander Lorantelle growled and reached for a data pad.

14 - Dinner and a Show

"Okay, Amanda," Chad said slowly, shoving his hands into his jeans pockets, chewing on his words as he searched for something appropriate to say.

Amy was pretty and he had no problems talking with her. On the other hand, Amanda was gorgeous—far prettier than any of the cheerleaders at the junior high school. He had never spoken to any of those girls and now found himself tongue-tied and unable to come up with anything clever or impressive to say to this one. Finally, he gave up and asked, "What do we do now?"

As the question passed his lips and before he could close his mouth, his stomach grumbled. The noise sounded somewhere been a frog croaking and a duck being run over by a motorcycle. Wishing he could somehow erase the embarrassing noise, he slapped his hand to his lips.

"I'd say, first, we need to find something to eat," Amanda said. Her beautiful dark eyes twinkled as she turned toward the dim kitchen. Chad followed, shaking his head.

They found meat, cheese, and crusty sourdough bread.

"Where's the rest of your family?" Chad asked the girl as they sat at the table. The bread was a little stale, but Chad was hungry enough not to care, and chewed off large bites of the sandwich.

"Oh, they're at home," she said casually.

Chad looked around the room as if he could have missed seeing others about.

Amanda laughed. "They're not here. We live in another dimension. Uncle Ted got a message to us saying you would be coming through, possibly this way, and it would be good if someone could meet up with you and maybe help you along. You know my uncle Ted, right? He's Amy's dad."

Chad dropped his piece of bread. "Amy's dad is here?" He looked around the room again and tried to think of what he should do next. "Can we go talk to him?

Maybe he can tell me what I need to do. How did he get here? I mean, I never saw him get past me."

"Slow down, Chad." Amanda rolled her eyes. "I never said he was here." She reached out and placed her hand on his. The light shock and tingle brought his attention back to her, and he looked into her dark, sympathetic eyes. Her mouth was slightly open and he could just see the tips of her two front teeth between her glistening red lips. His heart pounded with excitement.

"I'm sorry. I forgot you're not from the dimensions. I should explain more when I speak." Chad felt a moment of disappointment as she took her hand away from his and leaned back into her chair. "Uncle Ted had to come in by another route and is on the other side of what you might call a wall of the opposition. It would have been too dangerous to follow you, or even to come here, where you are now. He was able to get the message to me without alerting our enemies and that's why I searched you out."

"So, if you had to come find me, then this isn't your house?" Chad asked, more confused than ever.

"No." Amanda smiled from one side of her mouth. "I have no idea whose house this is. I knew which transitional path you had used from the prime dimension and found the spot where the gate you used had closed; they leave a resonant shadow on the ground below where they were. That's how I tracked you here."

Amanda stood and gathered the plates and flatware they had used and took them to the sink. As she washed the items, she continued, "Everyone, well, almost everyone has cleared out of this dimension, and several more between here and the battle lines. Most people only left a day or two ago. We're gathering to a safe place and working on our strategies."

She placed the dishes neatly in a cupboard and closed the door. When she looked back at Chad, lines of worry creased her brow. "The main problem is, if I could find you, then anyone else who figured out you came through that transitional dimension could find you too. We need to get on our way and take the fastest possible route out of here."

Amanda looked around the dining room and kitchen. "I'll need your help, and I'll need some tools. I hope these people have something I can use. You go back to the living room and try to get comfortable. You need to be as relaxed as possible for this to work."

"Great," Chad said. "Now I'll be too worried to relax."

He grabbed his backpack off a dining room chair and wandered back to the cozy room at the front of the house where he flopped onto a puffy cushioned couch, stretched his legs out and closed his eyes. He could hear Amanda sliding drawers open and closed in the rooms down the short hallway.

"Have you ever played one of these?" he heard Amanda ask, startling him. He must have fallen asleep. She held out a short silver object. Chad tried to place what the item was as his groggy thoughts fell back into their normal places.

"A harmonica?" he asked.

"Yes," she said. She closed her eyes and sighed. Her dimples deepened as she wrinkled her brow.

"Sorry," Chad said. "You told me to relax, and I'm afraid I did. But no, I've never played a harmonica. Do you want me to try to play a song?"

She threw him the small musical instrument. "No, I just want you to play a note. But it has to be perfect. That's why you need to be relaxed, not nervous. The note needs to be pure and unwavering. Look at the holes. There are numbers above them. Find hole number three and blow that one."

Chad gave it a try.

"Close," she said. "But you have to hit just one hole. Do this with your mouth. Like you're trying to blow out a single birthday candle." She puckered her lips until she made a small round hole and blew.

Chad's heart stopped a moment as he took in Amanda's glistening red lips, long eyelashes on half-closed eyes, her beautiful unblemished skin framed by her luxurious auburn hair. A tinkling melody, like small bells tapped lightly, echoed in the back of his mind as a trance settled over him. His eyelids drooped. He puckered his lips and leaned forward to kiss her. What would those glistening lips taste like?

"Chad," he heard a distant voice say. "Hello, Chad. Wake up."

Chad opened his eyes abruptly to find Amanda leaning away from him in her seat, a coy smile on her alluring lips. Embarrassed realization colored his face nearly as bright red as Amanda's lips. "Um, uh, I uh," Chad stammered.

Amanda cut him off with a wink. "Don't worry about it," she said. "Just try blowing the harmonica again."

"Right." He raised the harmonica to his lips while focusing on the third hole and blew lightly to find the correct note. Once he found the right hole, he gave it a solid blow as he tried to form a small circular opening with his mouth.

"Great. You're getting it," she said. "Now relax and just breathe. That will keep the note steady."

As he did, Amanda sang a progression of notes. He was reminded of the cat, Shadow, in the transitional dimension, when she had adjusted his sight by producing a combination of tones. As Amanda sang, for an instant, the entire wall behind her flashed gossamer-mother-of-pearl, but as quickly as it had appeared, the illusion faded.

"What was that?" Chad asked as he dropped the harmonica into his lap.

"We're trying to open a portal out of this dimension. I don't think we're safe here, and there's no time to fool around. Pulling up a portal is really hard when you only have two people, especially when one doesn't know what he's doing. Three is a piece of cake, but that's not an option right now. You have to relax and focus." She sounded annoyed. "We need to get to the place where everyone is gathering. It's safe there and I'd like to skip of few of the more dangerous areas in between, or at least have a say about which of the lands we pass through."

"Oh," Chad said, feeling sufficiently stupid. "I didn't know what you were doing and when the portal flashed right here in the room, I was a bit surprised. Let's try again."

He put the harmonica back to his mouth and blew a soft and steady note. He kept his eyes on the wall as Amanda sat on the end of the sofa. Back straight and eyes closed in concentration she sang the confusing melody again. Intermittent vague flashes of the swirling opalescence flickered before them, though none lasted longer than a few seconds. Eventually, Amanda threw herself back onto the thick, soft cushions of the couch and sighed as she looked up at the ceiling.

She had a beautiful neck, framed by her auburn hair sprawled across the cushion. Chad felt his arms and legs go weak and understood the temptation a vampire would have to sink his fangs into such a luscious neck.

"Um, Amanda?" Chad's throat felt like sand paper. He coughed lightly and asked. "So, what do we do now?"

"If Amy was here, we could sing together," she said as she sat back up and finger-combed her hair. "The two of us combined could compensate for your inconsistent tone. Really, with Amy here, we could pick a spot anywhere in the dimensions and open a portal right on top of it. She's that good."

"With Amy here, we wouldn't need to go anywhere but back to the real world," Chad said morosely. Amanda's smile soured as she squinted one of her eyes at him. He shrugged. "I mean, that's what I'm doing here, right? To bring her back?"

Amanda maintained her glare.

"Okay," he said to fill the suddenly heavy silence. "If I had a recorder, I could play a steady note. We had to play those all the time in sixth grade and I got pretty good."

Chad was shocked to see the happy, open expression return to Amanda's face as if night had turned to day in an instant.

"That's funny," she said. "The very first portal ever was opened almost a thousand years ago by two teenaged girls, cousins, of the aristocracy. They sang as a peasant boy played his flute. Those three were the first to enter the dimensions. The parallels are incredible, aren't they?"

It was Chad's turn to glare. "A peasant boy? You see a parallel there?"

Amanda wasn't fazed. "Sure. You're not a peasant, we don't have those anymore, but Amy and I are both from one of the oldest, most highly respected families that have ever lived in the dimensions. You're not."

"I am too. I just didn't know it until recently," Chad defended. "I'm a Lorantelle."

Amanda said nothing at first. She only looked at him, her head tipped forward like she was looking over eyeglasses that had slid down on her nose. She frowned.

"Who have you been talking to?" she asked, and shook her head like she was trying to clear cobwebs. "How do you know about Lorantelle?"

"My English teacher did a genetic scan on me, right after she figured out who Derrick was. She said I had like, a ninety-eight percent match to Lorantelle. I don't know what everyone is getting all worked up about. Mrs. Walker said it was a good name."

"Maybe it *was*," Amanda said. She looked sad, an air of defeat about her as she rose from the couch. "Grab your backpack and come on, we have a ways to go." Without another word, she headed for the door.

Out on the street, they turned up the dark sidewalk. Street lamps cast evenly spaced circles of light onto the walk and street as far down as they could see. Amanda stopped abruptly and turned to Chad.

"This all changed for me when you told me your name," she said, deep lines of concern furrowing her brow. "I don't know how you play into this. I don't know if you're an ally or an enemy to my cousin. I don't know if you really know. But right now, I need to get you to our headquarters and let the higher-ups figure it out."

"I don't care what you think of me," Chad said, defensive. "I know who I am and what I'm about. I'm Amy's friend. Sure, I'm the one that sent her into this mess, but I'm here to get her back out."

"Fine. We'll leave it at that, for now," Amanda said, resigned. "We need to get out of here. There's only one other person left in this dimension that might be able to help us. I don't entirely trust him, either, but he's our only choice at this point. We'll go to his place to see if he can get us a portal through to headquarters."

15 - A Walk in the Country

Chad followed Amanda in silence as they worked their way north through winding suburban streets. He felt like he was crowding her, so he slowed down until he hung back several paces. It felt good to be away from her, even if only a few yards. His head felt clearer, like a ringing in his ears had suddenly stopped.

Hulking sycamore silhouettes interspersed with ornate street lamps lined the neighborhood lanes. At times the two youths turned one way or another, but always found themselves eventually heading north again. A mostly full moon peeked over the tops of houses to the east, and hung, lopsided, over the horizon when they entered a country road and left the established town behind.

Chad thought about the past few hours—Amanda's sudden appearance, her relation to Amy, and their attempt at creating a portal. He was mystified that Amanda's reaction to his family name was the same as Shadow's, and his chest grew tight with frustration that the one connection he had to this world was turning out to be a hindrance, rather than a help.

It seemed a little convenient that Amanda was able to find him in all this open space—convenient and suspicious.

"Amanda," Chad said loud enough for her to hear. She stopped and turned. The moonlight's shadows made her face an eerie mask, her emotions effectively obscured by the darkness.

The pressure in Chad's head and ears returned as he approached the young woman.

"I'm confused," he confessed. "I don't know you, or if I can even trust you. But I don't really have a choice. I don't know where to go, and I can only hope you'll take me somewhere that will be better than where I was."

Her dark eyes remained unreadable.

"I thought I was doing the right thing, coming here to help my friend, but then found out who I'm related to and you acted like I'm the devil or something. You talked about Lorantelle like he or she was one person and not just a family. A family that was supposed to be good, according to my English teacher. She married a

Lorantelle, though I think her husband got killed a long time ago."

Amanda finally spoke. She leaned toward Chad, shook her head and whispered, "You don't know who Lorantelle is?"

"I just told you that." Chad allowed frustration to accent his words. "I know what it is. It's a family name. If there's more than that, you need to fill me in or get over it."

"Alright," Amanda said softly. "Come on. I'll tell you as we walk. It's going to take most the night to get where we're going I want to get there while it's still dark, so we can scope the place out safely."

She turned back up the narrow country road. Tall mounds of blackberries were dark walls in the yellow moonlight and stretched into the invisible distance on both sides.

Chad walked beside Amanda, listening as she spoke in a hushed, possibly fearful tone. "There was a man. Well, there is a man named Steven Lorantelle, who used to be on our side, the Starside. Well, we thought he was on our side. He was hard-working and well trusted, but pretty quiet. He just did his job like he was asked. No complaints, no arguments. Then one day about four years ago, people started disappearing—important people, people who knew our plans, our headquarters, and our personnel. It didn't take too long to find the common denominator was Lorantelle."

She walked in silence for a few yards, then laughed. "Well, I guess it did take too long, 'cause when they busted his door down to arrest him, only the faint residual energy of his exit portal remained. There wasn't much energy to read, but there was enough to know which direction he went—straight to the middle of Cloudland. It didn't make any sense to try to chase him. They knew where he was and no one was going to get close to him."

"So, this Steven guy disappeared and was never seen again?" Chad asked.

"Pretty much," Amanda agreed. "He was never seen in the open, or in Star lands. But our spies keep an eye on him and they say he was made a commander in the Cloud ranks. He's a ruthless interrogator. After he got away, our people researched him a bit. All they could find was he had come from the prime dimension about ten years ago. He was just a normal guy; no one paid him any attention."

"You wouldn't think one guy could ruin an entire family name," Chad said. "There must be other Lorantelles that are still good people, upholding the values of our name."

"Um, no," Amanda said. "There really aren't any Lorantelles around anymore. They all seem to have disappeared back into the prime dimension sometime between your First and Second World Wars."

Chad thought about it. Now there were only two Lorantelles left in the dimensions—this commander, and himself. He wanted to give Commander Lorantelle a piece of his mind, but what would he say? His mind was getting so dull and fuzzy.

The moon had climbed well into the sky when the broad, flat pastures beyond the blackberry hedges gave way to low rolling hills.

Chad cleared his throat.

"Can you tell me why my head feels all cloudy when you're close to me, and my ears ring like there's a lot of pressure in my head? At first, I thought I was in love, but I'm over that now. I noticed it when I dropped behind you to walk by myself for a while. The feeling went away, and then when you waited for me, it came back."

Amanda stopped walking suddenly and looked at Chad sideways, her head tilted at an angle.

"You're over me now, are you?" She said with one eyebrow raised. The evil smile on her face glowed in the direct light of the moon. Chad thought she was teasing him at first, but then a chill of warning ran up his spine.

"No, I guess I'm not really over you," he said more sheepishly than he wished, and wondered why he was even admitting this to her. "But you are scaring me with that look. Are you going to rip out my heart or suck my blood or something?"

The expression on Amanda's face softened immediately to alarmed contrition.

"I'm sorry, Chad," she said with believable sincerity. "I was just listening to your soul. It isn't easy, and people have told me before the strain makes me do weird faces."

"Listening to my soul?" Chad said, aghast. "And I thought having my blood sucked sounded horrifying. Are you going to suck out my soul?"

"Now you're being stupid," she said and continued walking. "I said I was *listening* to your soul. I'm not good at it, not like Amy is."

When Amanda paused Chad asked, "Is that why the Cloudside wants to control Amy? Because she's really good at making portals or reading souls? Is that what makes her the Star Daughter?"

"No. Casting portals and reading souls is something anyone who has the talent to manipulate energy can do. And the Star Daughter is just a title from an old prophecy. The Cloudside wants her because she's a diplomat. Hers is a special talent. It's rare and Amy appears to be the strongest one ever."

Chad shrugged. "Being diplomatic is good, I guess. I still don't see why the Cloudside would want to control that."

Amanda huffed. "You don't see because it is more than just being diplomatic. A diplomat in the dimensions is someone who can tell you what to do, and you have to do it. You want to do it, and will, no matter what. If the Cloudside got Amy on their side, she could command everyone in the dimensions to do what the Cloudside wants them to do."

Chad shook his head. "I don't see how anyone could make you *want* to do something against your will."

"Your will is an extension of your soul, and as I was saying, the soul is energy inside your physical body. Like light and sound, the energy gives off waves. If you tune your own soul, and you're good at it, you can read other souls. Amy can take it one step further and tune other souls to her. When you are aligned with a soul you can tell whether they are good or evil, strong or weak, if they have the talent to bend energy to open a portal and live in the dimensions, or if they are just dull, untalented primers."

"So, am I a dull primer?" Chad asked, expecting to hear he was. "I've lived in the prime dimension my whole life."

"No," Amanda said, her voice serious. "I'm the dull one. I hadn't considered it before. I assumed you were just a primer and I didn't put two and two together, even when you told me you're a Lorantelle."

She stopped walking again and placed her hand on his arm. The familiar electric tingle vibrated against his skin where her fingertips touched. "Like I said, Amy's the one who can read souls. I'm not. But I think you must be powerful. As the Star Daughter's Champion you should have the ability to turn the talents of others back on them in defense of Amy. As Champion, you may be the only one in the dimensions with the ability to resist the Star Daughter's commands.

"The pressure you feel when you're close to me is probably interference. Like the sound a microphone makes when it gets in a feedback loop. You're getting feedback from my soul."

"So how do I tune my own soul, to listen to yours or anyone else?" Chad asked.

"Maybe you are a dull primer," Amanda muttered cheerfully. "I've said twice already I'm not good at it. And even if I was, it's really hard to describe. To me, it's like when you're going up into the mountains and your ears start to plug. If you drop your jaw it opens up your ears and the pressure equalizes and suddenly you hear clearly again. You have to do kind of the same thing with your soul. You relax it, or tighten it up, and the pitch changes. When your pitch aligns with another person's you'll almost see into their mind. Or maybe it's their heart you see into, because all of their feelings flow into you. You know their true intentions."

The blackberry hedges tapered off as they worked their way up a small hill. The road wound around it to the left. As they followed the long curve of the road, far in the distance they saw a small cottage at the bottom of a cleft between two of the treeless hills. The short grass on the hillside was brown in the yellow light of the moon.

Amanda stopped in her tracks, taking hold of his arm so he would stop as well. "Get down and be quiet," she hissed and indicated a low rock wall.

"Whose house is that?" Chad murmured.

"He's an old man named Brendan Thrush. Now get down here like I told you," she growled at him quietly.

Chad crouched behind the girl and watched her in silence. She chewed her lower lip as she peered across the long, shallow draw near the cottage. Dim light shimmered in the single visible window. As he considered Amanda, Chad mentally dropped his jaw and relaxed a point within his head where he felt the most tension. The pressure and dullness he had felt while in Amanda's presence dissipated rapidly, as if he had stepped far enough away from the girl to be unaffected by her soul. Yet, where the dullness and pressure had been, there was now an overwhelming sense of anxiety combined with fear for Amy's safety, a distrust of the man who resided in the cottage, and a general feeling of insecurity about everything around them.

Amanda turned suddenly, as if Chad had just pinched her.

"What are you doing?" she whispered. Her voice hissed like an angry snake.

"Sorry," Chad said and scooted back from her. "I didn't think it would actually work. I just thought it might help me relax."

"Well, be careful," she said and turned back to look at the cottage. "If you haven't practiced reading souls, a lot, and you try to tap into someone, they can catch you doing it. When you tap into another person, your own emotions and intentions might bleed forward and give you away. The person you're reading can read you in return. If we get into that house over there, keep your thoughts to yourself, or you may get us into trouble."

"Okay," Chad said with barely controlled sarcasm, "I have no idea what I just did, but I'll try not to do it again."

16 - A (not so) Friendly Chat

"Come on." Amanda stood and waved her hand toward the cottage. "I don't think there's anyone with him in there. If he's in a good mood and we're polite we should be able to get him to help us, without him charging us a lot."

"There are two things that worry me about your plan," Chad whispered as they turned up the long gravel driveway that led from the road to Thrush's house. "One: if anyone woke me up at this time of night, there is no way I would be in a good mood. And two: I hope you have some money, because if he wants to charge us even five bucks, that's more than I have."

"You don't need to worry about waking him up. I don't think he ever sleeps. He actually uses the time of day as a bargaining chip. Coming at this time, he'll think he has the upper hand. That's also why you don't need to worry about money. He barters and bargains for everything, and his unit of exchange is favors. If you wake him at night, he factors it into the exchange. If you interrupt his work during the day, and I hear he always says he was working, he factors that in as well. Fortunately, he owes my family a small favor, so we start out with points on our side."

"Favors?" Chad asked. "That sounds too much like the mob. How do you know we can trust this guy? Someone who deals in favors sounds like he belongs on the Cloudside."

"I know it sounds like we're working with the enemy, but he treats everyone equally, Starside and Cloudside alike. That's why he's still out here after everyone else has evacuated. Both sides owe him favors. If either side came down on him, he has enough leverage with important people to push it right back in their faces."

They were close enough to the house to see the windows were open. The curtains stirred lazily on the slight breeze. Amanda stopped, knelt on one knee, and motioned for Chad to do the same.

"Don't say anything to Brendan," Amanda whispered. "I'll tell him you're my dull cousin, and you got left behind in the exodus. I came back to find you and the portal closed before I could get us back through. Since no one can raise a portal by themselves, and since you're dull, he should accept the story pretty easily and help us out."

"Dull cousin, huh?" Chad was annoyed. "Maybe I should drool to make it more convincing."

"Oh, I don't think that will be necessary," Amanda said dismissively. "Just try to look bored. Stare at the ground a lot, and avoid looking Brendan in the eyes. And for heaven's sake, don't try to read his soul."

"Right." He realized then, the pressure he had felt in his head whenever he was close to her was completely gone. It had disappeared when he had tried to tune himself, and it hadn't returned.

"Right," Chad said again. "Whenever you're ready."

Amanda nodded her head and her auburn curls bounced and shimmered in the moonlight.

Chad stood behind her as she knocked on the warped wooden door. Luminescent slivers shone through the gaps in the frame and burst suddenly into a dazzling supernova as Brendan jerked the door open. Light flooded the porch from within.

"Do they have giants in the dimensions?" Chad tried to ask as he clasped his head with both hands.

Brendan Thrush's silhouette filled the open doorway and towered over the two teens. Chad looked up and then away and tried to focus on the ground as the familiar pressure hammered inside his head. If the man in the doorway had boxed Chad's ears, the pain wouldn't have been worse than the pressure inside his skull from merely standing this close to the powerful man. Chad bent over with his hands on his ears and groaned.

"What's wrong?" Amanda gasped.

He kept his eyes down, shook his head and droned in a monotone, "I'm okay."

"What do you want, girl?" the man snapped at Amanda.

"Good evening, Mr. Thrush," she said cheerfully. "I'm in need of a favor."

"A favor at this hour may be difficult to come by," Brendan said, his voice a slow rasp against rotten wood. "But come in and we'll see if you can be accommodated."

"Thank you, Mr. Thrush," her voice dripped with gratitude.

She turned to Chad and gestured him forward. She spoke as a child would to a doll, "Come Ch—Charles. Don't be afraid. This man won't hurt you. He can help us. He can get us back home. You want to see your mother, don't you, Charles?"

Thrush bent forward to avoid hitting his head as he passed through the arched entrance to the sitting room. Amanda followed. Thrush folded himself onto a wooden chair, his bony knees high above the seat, almost to his ears as he leaned forward to stare at the two youths. For all his frightening demeanor, he looked like a giant grasshopper who had been invited to a formal dinner and forced to sit in a chair as a human would. Amanda walked Chad to a couch and sat him at one end while she sat in the middle, on the edge of the cushion. With her back straight and hands folded in her lap she was the picture of a demure young business woman. She smiled at the old man who scrubbed at the short, silver-white whiskers that grew thick on his jowls.

The pressure in Chad's head became almost unbearable. He imagined a large clamp squeezing his head, the dial twisting to increase its tightness. Though he struggled against the agony, he did his best to maintain his focus on the floor in front of him and listen to Amanda and Thrush. Their voices rose and fell as they spoke. At times Chad imagined he heard repeating melodies and rhythms within their words and phrases, as if each tone and inflection held intent and hidden meaning.

As his mind wandered and wrapped itself around the strange undertones and counter melodies of Amanda and Thrush's verbal chess game, he found a place in the back of his head, like a child stumbling into an unknown room in his own home. Standing in this safe spot, he reached out with his mind. Barely perceptible even to himself, he found the edge of the pressure and pushed against it. The pain eased.

Chad turned his attention back to the conversation. Neither Amanda nor Brendan appeared to have noticed the change he felt and continued their jockeying for position in their negotiations. Another gentle push in the back of his brain and the pain in his ears was all but gone.

He sighed with relief.

Amanda said, "What we need is a portal into, or near, our headquarters. I would understand if you weren't able to pop one open right on top our general's tent. It is pretty well protected. But it's well known which dimension it's in and I'm sure the two of us could open a passage close to the dimensional border."

Chad felt Thrush go cold and wondered if Amanda had baited him intentionally. He hoped the barb had worked but feared the girl had overstepped herself. If he was offended, the giant didn't say.

"The boy is of no use?" Brendan asked, "We would do much better to have three."

"No," Amanda shook her head. "As the saying goes, 'If he knew what day it was he could open a portal by himself.' But he's hopeless. The best we can do is you and me together."

Chad felt Thrush's eyes on him, and fought to maintain the appearance of disinterest, his eyes on the floor. The air in the room turned colder still and Chad considered which way to run if he suddenly had to escape the cottage.

"Come, then," Thrush said abruptly and stood. "We will open the portal on this wall. You will only have a few seconds to get through. I can picture some do-gooder seeing the foreign portal open up near your headquarters and think they are saving the world by collapsing it back on me, so be ready."

Amanda helped Chad to his feet and stood with him, facing the wall. Thrush began with low tones, shuffling them around like pieces of a wooden puzzle. When he reached a specific point in his note progressions, he raised his hand and held it above his head. Chad and Amanda watched until he brought the hand down quickly and pointed at Amanda. She began the tonal progressions, but in her own range. At times she modulated with Thrush's notes and at times harmonized.

Chad felt energy building in the room. He could sense where the portal would open. Like the vortex of a whirlwind, it pulled him toward the wall. With a rush of wind and the scream of torn fabric, time and space shifted and the portal burst into the room, just inches from where they stood.

Amanda grabbed Chad's arm, pulled him toward the portal, and shouted, "Let's go."

"No," Chad pulled back, and shook free of Amanda's grasp. "It's wrong. The portal is wrong."

Icy wind blew from the center of the swirling, shimmering disk. The pressure returned in Chad's head and threatened to blast open his skull. Though the pain in his ears rang like church bells on Christmas day he could hear the fundamental chord progressions of the portal. And what he heard wasn't good.

"We have to go," Amanda screamed again. She took his arm with both her hands and pulled him forward. As he tried to break free of her a second time, Chad felt hands land firmly on his back, and shove him forward into an icy, swirling void.

17 - An Early Morning Exchange

Commander Lorantelle waited on the inlaid mosaic patio outside the main entrance to the Chateau and pondered the early morning sky. The dazzling array of stars spread across the black velvet expanse and only faded slightly at the very edge of the eastern horizon.

Still hours before dawn, he thought, and breathed deeply of the warm Mediterranean air. He had tried to sleep, but couldn't. After wrestling with the bed sheets for several hours he felt a walk around the grounds might at least calm his thoughts.

It was good to be alone. In reality, they were probably watching him at the very moment, but at least he could revel in the illusion of privacy and be himself, if only for a few moments. He walked down the few short stone steps that took him to the broad manicured lawn and across to the low wall where Lord Caltone's servant had found him the day before. In the valley far below, cattle lowed in the darkness. No doubt a farmer had just begun his long, tedious day.

The thought of the farmer's pointless drudgery jarred Lorantelle's memory back to what had kept him awake through so many recent nights. It really didn't make sense that one man, himself in this case, could have so much power and spend his days primarily at leisure, all because of the random dispensation of a mental gift. The *ungifted* farmer in the valley below must carry out his labor manually. Meanwhile, if Lorantelle had the compunction, and a friend or two, he could generate a glass of milk with a few casual notes.

Caltone called it a birth right—his highness having the greatest share. "You and I have been given this gift," he had pontificated to Lorantelle when they first met. "It is not only our right to use it for our personal improvement, but it is our responsibility to establish ourselves as holders of the power, and thereby the authority, which we do possess. To assume the laborer, the un-gifted, or untalented are equal to ourselves, or entitled to the benefits we possess is contrary to the natural laws."

Lorantelle hadn't responded to Caltone's dissertation, other than to bow himself out of his leader's chambers with a respectful, "Yes, my lord."

The dimensions had been discovered a thousand years before by the children of a land owner in what would become France. When and why un-gifted residents were introduced to the dimensions was impossible to say. Maybe some gifted aristocrat couldn't live without his serfs surrounding him and reminding him of his own import. Common labor wasn't needed. But the commoners were here now, and they couldn't be evicted back to the Prime Dimension without revealing to the rest of the world the dimensions' existence.

Lorantelle's own talent, though he had never discussed it with the egocentric, self-proclaimed dimensional leader, was more than merely the skill of verbal coercion. Many a strong-willed, and mentally talented Cloudsider had caved to his interrogation and spilled safely guarded military secrets. Though he was a skilled orator and convincing debater, the true basis for his success lay in his ability to bend sound and energy within his opponent's mind to elicit feelings of fear, dread, and hopelessness. Some of his victims took time to break, others caved almost immediately, but all left their encounter a crumpled, empty husk of their former selves.

All except for one. The girl had been impervious to his inquisition, her mind protected by a seemingly impenetrable shell. Rather, it was more a mirror; the energy had been repelled. It was unlike anything he had seen before, and it had shaken his confidence.

"What right do I have to interfere with the minds and lives of these people?" he muttered to himself. "Or to keep them subjected. Feudalism ended centuries ago."

"Commander." The unexpected voice of Felipe from behind him made Lorantelle jump slightly.

He spun on his heel, hoping the ambient starlight was dim enough to not betray the surprise and chagrin written across his face. Had the young man heard his mumbled self-doubt?

"Felipe," he snapped. "What do you want? Why can't I be left alone once in a while?"

"I'm sorry, commander," Felipe stammered, "His High..., Lord Caltone requests your presence. He says he has news of an important development. You weren't in your rooms, and I have been looking for you for almost an hour now."

The poor boy's voice shook as he wrung his hands and shifted back and forth.

"Felipe," the commander said sternly yet with a note of compassion. "Pull yourself together. Come. I will speak to Lord Caltone, and explain why you had difficulty finding me. He can't punish you for carrying out his orders."

#

"Enter," Caltone called when Lorantelle knocked soundly on the ornately carved wooden door.

"Wait out here, Felipe," Lorantelle said to the servant. "If his highness wants you, he can call for you himself."

Lorantelle closed the door behind him and strode purposefully toward the Cloudside's highest leader. He spoke as he walked, "I tried to find some seclusion in your grand domicile, yet your tenacious messenger was still able to interrupt my personal reflection."

Caltone's smile was smug as he replied, "Yes. Felipe is persistent when given a task. You'll have to forgive the offense. It was at my request."

"Yes, my lord," the commander replied with a small nod as he came to a stop before Caltone's broad ebony desk. He waited for the supreme leader to speak.

"The hour is late," Caltone began after a short pause. "I will get right to this. I have received a communication that your quarry has been, shall we say, sequestered, by an associate of mine. He has agreed to hold the boy until you can take charge of him."

The Cloudside lord was silent for a time and merely stared at Lorantelle as if awaiting a response. The commander raised his eyebrows.

Caltone scowled and said, "I want you there as soon as possible. I will have three portal agents meet you in the lobby in one hour to open a passage for you that should place you within easy walking distance of my associate. Do you have any questions?"

"Only two. Does your associate have a name? And may I ask Felipe to perform a few small tasks in my absence?"

"My associate's name is Brendan Thrush," Caltone said, eyes narrowed, but the commander knew nothing of the man and maintained a look of passing interest.

"Thank you," Lorantelle replied with a partial bow, then asked, "And your boy?"

"By all means," Caltone said with an air of indifference and dismissal. "You may go."

"Yes, my lord," Lorantelle said and left the room.

Back outside the ornate door, Felipe leaned against the wall, dozing. The commander took hold of the boy's shirt sleeve as he strode past and half dragged him along as he hurried down the hallway.

"I have a task for you, Felipe," Lorantelle said when they were well away from Caltone's chambers. "I'll be leaving in an hour and I wish to speak to you and Derrick before I go. Find him and bring him to my room in a quarter hour."

As they entered the lobby and passed Julia's vacant reception desk, Felipe asked, "What if he won't come? Derrick is currently asleep."

The commander stopped and looked over the desk to ascertain if there were any visible intercoms or other listening devices. When he could find none, he told the boy, "You have fifteen minutes. Prove to me I can depend on you. Now go."

As the boy hurried off, Lorantelle headed to his own chambers to gather his traveling gear, and his thoughts.

#

It took twenty minutes, but Lorantelle had to give Felipe credit for his success as he dragged the taller boy into the commander's chambers. Derrick wore nothing but sweat pants and an irritated, though groggy, expression.

"That was much easier than I thought," Felipe said with a smirk. "I don't think he even woke up until we were almost here."

"Good work, Felipe," the commander said.

Derrick dragged in a deep breath as if to begin a diatribe, but Lorantelle held up his hand to forestall any comment. "I don't have much time, and no desire for discussion. I am going away for most of the day and won't be able to make the changes I had planned to implement once the staff has awoken."

He folded the piece of parchment he had been writing on, sealed it with a gold sticker and wrote his name across the oak-leaf stylized seal. "Felipe, give this letter to Julia. In it are instructions authorizing the two of you to move the girl to more pleasant accommodations. There is a small room off the main corridor that can be locked, with no other exits, and a bathroom of its own. Once she is in that room, Felipe, you will be personally and singularly responsible for her care. Food, water and reasonable requests will be carried out immediately."

Derrick, completely awake by then, spluttered, "You can't do that. She's a prisoner. We have her where we want her and we'll lose all the ground we've made if you change that now."

Lorantelle got to his feet, picked up a small leather backpack and slung it over his shoulder. "We have gained no ground with this girl, Derrick, and with every hour she remains tied to a chair in the wine cellar, her resolve against us strengthens. You struck on the answer yesterday. She must *want* to join us, but she will never do so if we maintain our current tactics."

He turned and headed for the door. "We'll make her comfortable, and I will speak to her when I return. I should have additional options to persuade her when I next confront her."

He led the two boys into the lobby. "Derrick, after you assist Felipe in getting the girl to her new room, you are to have no contact with her at all. Felipe, choose a young woman you can trust. If you need assistance with our guest, or need relief from your watch, she may provide it for you."

Derrick sneered at Lorantelle. "You can't tell me what to do. Especially if you're not even going to be here. I'll tell Caltone..."

The commander didn't even look at the insolent boy, simply closed his eyes and listened to the tone of the teen's words until he found a cadence in Derrick's diction. Lorantelle hummed a counter melody to the notes hidden within the boy's words, and turned the energy of the sound against him.

Derrick abruptly stopped talking and twitched his head as if flipping hair from his eyes. A moment later, he twitched again and rubbed the back of his neck with one hand while he took three rapid, panting breaths. Derrick visibly paled and sweat broke out across his pasty brow. The commander stopped humming and relaxed his grip on the boy's mind.

"*Lord* Caltone," Lorantelle stressed to the young man, "has already turned the disposition of the prisoner over to me and should not be bothered by any trivialities you mistakenly think might be important."

Derrick inhaled to speak, but stopped and looked toward the main entrance as three men entered the lobby and acknowledged the commander.

"You have your orders," Lorantelle told Derrick and Felipe as he followed the men out the door and into the warm blackness of early morning.

18 - Cat and Cat.

Lorantelle followed the men down the stairs toward the lawn where they stopped at the edge of the dewy grass. One of the men stood next to each of the stairway's stone balustrades, while the third remained next to the commander.

"I'm Warrant Officer Childers, commander," he said as he turned toward Lorantelle. "We will open a portal within one hundred meters of Thrush's place and reopen the portal for a few minutes every hour until you return."

"Thank you, Officer Childers," Lorantelle said formally.

Lorantelle remained silent as the three men of the summoning detail began an intricate chant. The warrant officer held long low notes as those to the sides intoned alternating and conflicting progressions. Reflexively he identified the patterns and variations of each of the men and considered how the sounds could be twisted and turned against them to induce fear and pain.

A gossamer disk burst into existence a half meter from where they stood.

The commander looked through the portal and studied the scene before him—low, undulating fields of star-lit grass and broadly scattered oak trees. A gravel road wound leisurely into the distance around a squat, low hill. In a far-off draw, a speck of light identified the location of Thrush's home.

Lorantelle's boots crunched on the gravel road as he stepped through the portal and walked up the dark lane. Dawn rapidly approached and the skyline was edged with rosy purple as he pounded on Thrush's hollow front door. Lights were on throughout the house, though there was no sign or sound of movement within. Impatient, he huffed in frustration as he pounded on the door a second time. When there was still no response, the commander leaned off the porch to get a better look through an open window into the empty sitting room.

"May I help you?" an unusually tall, skeletal man said from the open doorway.

Lorantelle turned to address the man. "Yes," the commander spoke gruffly, "Lord Caltone said you have a prisoner for me. I have come to retrieve him."

"A prisoner?" Thrush said with a frown and tapped his chin with a finger. He squeezed his cheeks together, pursing up his lips as if contemplating the idea, and added, thoughtfully, "Come to retrieve him?"

"Yes," Lorantelle said, his anger and impatience rising. "I need to retrieve him and be on my way. I'm a busy man and standing on this broken-down porch in this obscure dimension is accomplishing nothing."

"A busy man," Thrush said, and continued to squeeze his cheeks, giving him the appearance of a kissing fish in an aquarium.

It was too much for Lorantelle. "If it is your intention to merely repeat everything I say, try repeating this. 'Yes, Commander Lorantelle, I will go get the prisoner now.'"

The glimmer of irritation only lasted a moment as it flashed across Thrush's face. His expression returned to disinterested amusement, though he stopped squeezing his cheeks and slowly lowered his hand.

"Come in, commander," Thrush said and turned into the house. "I've brewed some tea. Do me the honor of sharing a cup?"

Lorantelle closed the front door behind himself and followed the tall, lanky man into the dingy kitchen. It seemed this man, Thrush, was more interested in playing mind games than in sharing anything useful to the alliance. Though Lorantelle had little patience for such, he would not allow this bizarre recluse to believe he had the upper hand.

They sat at a small wooden table so old the finish had been worn away in several places. Faded wallpaper from a forgotten era, peeling at corners and seams, was the only decoration in the dim dining room. Thrush poured tea into mismatched, chipped porcelain tea cups, smiled at his guest, and said, "So nice of you to visit me at such an unusual time of the morning."

Lorantelle considered the man's eccentric behavior and weighed how to approach the absurd opening comment. "Yes. It is quite early. My mission is important and requires us both to bear a little inconvenience."

"Inconvenience." Thrush rolled the word around in his mouth as though savoring a fine wine. "We must all pay the price of inconvenience, at times."

"It must be inconvenient, living out here, away from everything," Lorantelle commented dryly.

"Yes." Thrush looked the commander directly in the eyes, and said without his normal air of distraction. "I want all who come here to be prepared to pay the price for my services. If I am too easily found, people don't appreciate the cost."

"Indeed," Lorantelle said, distracted. He had already lost interest in small talk and wished only to be done with his business here. "Just coming out here should be payment enough."

"What are you willing to pay, commander?" Thrush asked, his gaze now icy and cutting.

"I pay?" Lorantelle asked, surprised. "Nothing. If you seek payment, you should speak with Lord Caltone."

The giant of a man half-closed his eyes, returning to his dreamy voice, "I am doing you a favor, Commander Lorantelle. I am providing you with the solution to all of your problems. The key, as it were, to your success or failure. That favor should be worth something to you."

The commander listened closely as Thrush spoke, following the rhythm and melody of the man's words until he found the cadence, and said, "You have done nothing for me. You have done me no favors. I will find whom I seek, with or without your help. I owe you nothing."

The chair beneath him creaked as Thrush sat up to his full height. His head appeared to brush the ceiling. "You will find him yourself?" Thrush grunted a cold, humorless laugh. "You cannot find him where I have put him. I alone can retrieve your little key. You think that is of no value? You should be–" He cut off with a jerk.

The commander's eyes narrowed as he hummed quietly. He picked up his tea cup and sniffed its contents before taking a sip.

Thrush jerked his head abruptly as if he had been slapped. He stared straight ahead, his eyes glazed. The tall man panted heavily and squeezed the heels of his hands against his temples. He shifted about in his chair as if unable to decide whether to stand or sit. Sweat beaded across the top of his balding head and quickly formed rivulets that ran down his cheeks and off his nose.

Lorantelle stopped humming and looked up to the other man's pale, clammy face. "Have you tired of our game, Thrush?"

"Yes. Yes," Thrush gasped and slumped down in the small wooden chair that groaned under his shifting weight. He held one hand to his heart and panted as he glared at the commander.

"Good." Lorantelle stood. "I'll give you a moment to compose yourself, but I do have commitments I must attend to."

Lorantelle stepped into the short hallway between the kitchen and the sitting room, his back to Thrush, and waited. He heard the other man push back the rickety chair and get to his feet. When he heard Thrush stop behind him, he turned his head slightly and spoke over his shoulder, "Good. Where have you sequestered the prisoner?"

Thrush dragged his feet as he pushed past Lorantelle into the narrow hallway. "Follow me."

They stood side by side in the sitting room and faced the wall. "Follow my lead and take the second variation from my pattern. I will point when you are to begin."

Lorantelle inhaled deeply to focus his mind and noted the patterns Thrush used varied slightly from the standard portal summoning at obscure points in his melody. Lorantelle joined in when Thrush indicated and sang standard progressions and counter melodies as established and taught to those with the skill to manipulate energy.

The portal burst into existence against the wall as it had hours earlier.

"They're in there," Thrush said. "Locked between dimensions. They are in an unconscious stasis, immobile. You need only reach your hand in and they may be drawn out."

"Do the honors," Lorantelle said and indicated the swirling black portal with the wave of his hand.

"By all means," Thrush said, eyebrows raised. "There is no need to be dubious. It is not a trap for you or me."

"Forgive me," Lorantelle muttered. "I question the veracity of anyone who would ransom a prisoner. To expect payment from Lord Caltone is bad enough, but your attempt to further pad your wallet at my expense warned me you are not to be trusted."

Thrush shrugged and stepped forward. He sank his hand and arm up to his shoulder in the opalescent black. His expression of pained indifference turned slowly to shock as he swayed from side to side, searching the portal for the two youths. He whirled back to Lorantelle. "Hold me by my belt and don't let go. I'm going to lean in for a look. If I step through, the portal will close on me. I and your prisoners will be locked in there forever."

"That's interesting. Only a moment ago you assured me this wasn't a trap for either of us," Lorantelle said dryly. He took hold of the giant's belt, braced his feet to hold the giant's weight. "You can't know the temptation you have presented me. I could dispose of my foe, and you, with a single push. Check quickly before I lose my self-control."

Thrush leaned his upper body forward through the shimmering, oily surface until his entire torso disappeared into the portal. The commander held tightly to the other man's belt as Thrush swayed his body back and forth, searching inside the portal. After a time, he became still. Lorantelle's muscles began to burn and he wondered if Thrush had become stuck or perhaps had suffocated in the icy swirling portal.

Thrush leaned back, suddenly, and reemerged from the darkness. His face was much paler, and his eyes appeared shocked and hollow.

"There is no explanation," Thrush said as he broke free of Lorantelle's grasp and turned to face the shorter, younger man. "This is impossible. They are not in the dimensional chamber."

"You're a fool and a failure," Lorantelle growled. Frustration and anger boiled in him, begging to be released. "And you will pay for your foolishness."

Planting his feet he grabbed Thrush by the lapels to unbalance him, and shoved the tall wraith of a man into the eternal darkness of the prison he had created.

19 - Dancing in the Dark

Chad woke in the absolute blackness of the dimensional chamber. Music like freeform jazz drifted quietly from all directions at once. He couldn't identify what instrument played the riffs which varied in rhythm and length. At times it could be a saxophone, and then at times a piano or organ—maybe a keyboard or synthesizer that could change its sound with the press of a button. Yet, underlying the unpredictable and confusing phrases, there remained a slow and constant chord progression. Chad found himself humming the notes as he considered his current situation.

Alarmed, he suddenly remembered how he had arrived there, in the dark. Someone, probably Thrush, had pushed him through a portal. It had felt wrong, evil, from outside, and he couldn't understand how Amanda had been so cavalier about charging into it. Though now, inside was peaceful and calming. Was this a trick, or a trap to hold him here passively? Make him a willing prisoner?

He didn't want to stay, but he also didn't feel threatened. He knew, somehow, he could leave the chamber when he wanted.

"Amanda?" Chad asked when his thoughts turned back to his companion. She had been right at his side when they entered the portal. As he spoke, the music abruptly faded. In fact, it had become so quiet he could hear the long, deep breaths of the girl beside him. With the sound of her breath came the faint bell melody he had heard back at the house where he had met her.

"Amanda, are you awake?" He turned toward the sound of her breaths and reached out, blindly.

And quickly jerked back his hands as they found part of Amanda he shouldn't grab hold of without permission. She was much closer than he expected, uncomfortably close, and he took a large step back to give her space.

He pictured where she would be after his adjustment. She was facing him, her right shoulder almost touching his chest. With this in mind he reached out again, aiming higher and toward where he assumed her shoulders would be. She hadn't moved. Or he hadn't.

He tried to push away. He felt his feet move, yet his upper body remained where it was. No matter how many steps he took in any direction, he remained next to her.

A soft puff of air tickled the hairs on the side of his face as Amanda exhaled. The tinkling sound of bells grew louder and control of his conscious mind seemed to slip a bit. Chad thought about those lips and remembered their lush redness as they puckered invitingly when she tutored him in playing the harmonica. He licked his own lips as his breathing quickened.

She was so close.

It would take only a moment to lean forward and discover if those lips felt as inviting as they had looked. He knew he shouldn't—it's not right to take advantage of a girl in such a situation. What would his mother say?

The bell melody sounded simultaneously distant and close at hand. It drowned out what remained of the room's ambient music and seemed to take over his mind—dulling it to all thoughts but Amanda.

As if they had a will of their own, he suddenly found his hands on Amanda's hips, his lips pressed to hers. As they touched, her lips parted slightly in response. Her breath tasted sweet and fresh, like strawberries and lemon-lime soda.

He didn't know what to do next. He had never kissed a girl before, other than his mother, and wasn't really sure what the process was. He had daydreamed about kissing Amy.

Amy. With a snap, the bell music stopped and Chad remembered where he was and why.

He was here to help his friend. But at the moment he was essentially in the arms of her cousin. He was immediately filled with guilt.

"Chad?" Amanda asked. "What are you doing?"

Sick with embarrassment he jerked back as best he could.

"Amanda," he gasped. "I'm sorry. You were asleep and..."

That sounded terrible. He felt like a creep—he was a creep.

"I'm sorry," he said again. "I didn't know what I was doing."

"That's the truth," Amanda said, a tinkling note of humor sneaking between her words. "That's about the worst kiss I've ever gotten. Good thing I wasn't Sleeping Beauty. That kiss would have woken Dozing Ugly."

Chad didn't know how to respond. As he searched for something to say, Amanda asked, "Where are we?"

"I hoped you would know," he replied. Irritation replaced chagrin as he remembered their situation. "You seemed so happy to jump into this portal, even when I told you it seemed wrong."

"I did?" she asked, sounding first surprised, then peeved. "Well, no. I wasn't *happy* to jump in here, if that's how you want to say it."

"Then what was it?" he asked. "It was almost like you knew we would be stuck in here and from where I'm standing, it looks like that was your plan."

"No, Chad." Her words sounded as angry as he felt. "It was not my plan to get us trapped in here, or anywhere for that matter. I just assumed you weren't familiar with how a portal should look and were probably just scared to enter it."

Chad wanted to believe her, but some undertone in her words—perhaps a rhythm to the way she spoke, or the way she articulated—something about them didn't ring true.

"So, how are we supposed to get out?"

"I'm not sure," Amanda mumbled, barely loud enough for Chad to hear. The ambient music had returned and it drifted about the chamber like water sloshing around a fish bowl. At times the music was soft and sounded as if it came from a distance. At other times it was louder and close by. But it was always present.

"I think we're in a dimensional chamber," she said, thoughtfully and a bit louder. "Can you sit down?"

"No. I've tried, but it keeps forcing me back up to a standing position."

Amanda reached out and touched his arm. "You wait here. I'm going to try to walk around. Keep talking to me, so I can orient myself to where you are."

"Right. What am I supposed to talk about?" Chad muttered. "Um, how about the music they pipe in here? If this is some kind of trap, why would they play us music? To keep us entertained and happy so we'll stay where we are? I mean, it's nice, but I still don't want to stay in here forever."

"Well," she said, still sounding close by where she had been before, "you don't have any problems coming up with something to talk about. It seems like you can talk forever."

"Yeah," he said, too preoccupied with Amanda's walking around experiment to feel insulted. "So how far away could you get before you ran into the edge of this chamber?"

"Nowhere," she said. Chad heard the disappointment in her voice. "I stayed in the same spot the whole time. No matter how much you move, you stay right where you are. It's like the dimension folds back in on itself and every step you take away is a step right back."

Chad wished he could see Amanda's face to try to read her eyes or her expression, to know if she was telling the truth. "How do we get out, then?"

Amanda sighed. "We don't. Not until someone comes and pulls us out."

"Great. We can't walk out. We can't sit down. But at least we have music. If we get too bored we can always dance. Though it doesn't really have a very good rhythm to dance to."

"What are you talking about?" Amanda asked, her words clipped and angry.

"Sorry," Chad said. "Just trying to keep it light." Then he thought about her words. "Don't you hear any music?"

"No," she sounded thoughtful again. "What does it sound like?"

"It's really hard to describe. There are lots of notes running around. At times they seem random. But there is an undercurrent, kind of a melody that goes, 'Bum, bum, bum, bum, bum.'"

"You can hear that?" Amanda asked.

"Sure. I think it's what woke me up. Can't you hear it?"

"No, I can't." Her voice was small and barely audible to Chad above the ambient music.

"Do it again," Amanda said. "But keep going this time."

"Well, that's about it," he said. "It does that a bit longer and then repeats. Here. It's starting again. Bum, bum, bum, bum, bum...."

"Chad," Amanda said, her voice full of hope. "This is the primary melody to generate a portal. Keep doing that. I want to try something."

"Okay," Chad said and started repeating the melody along with the music he heard. He made it through the entire strain before Amanda joined in with the counter.

She began with long notes that almost matched what Chad intoned, then broke off in a variety of rapid counters and variations of the primary.

Chad stopped. "No. That's not it. It sounds completely different."

Amanda gasped. "Don't stop, Chad. It sounds different because it is different. You must be hearing the melody and counter melody of the dimension we are in. My music sounds different because I'm trying to use the primary, which defines all portals, to call another portal to get us out."

She paused a moment as if gathering her thoughts. "I'm sorry. What I'm trying to get you to do is pretty advanced even for someone who grew up in the dimensions. But if you can maintain the primary melody, accurately, for a few minutes, I should be able to build us a portal out of here. You need to stay on key, in rhythm, and consistent. Do you think you can do that?"

"Sure," Chad said. "The more I follow that basic melody, the louder it gets. I should be able to stay with it. Just tell me when to start."

"Start whenever you're ready. I'll follow you. Just don't stop."

Chad listened for a moment to find a good starting point, then began. The melody had become so familiar he was able to anticipate the notes in order. He was so absorbed in the progression he hardly noticed Amanda join in. Rather than stumbling on the differences between what she sang and the organic melody of the dimensional chamber, he relaxed and allowed his melodic structure to mesh with the counter melodies she created. It sounded so beautiful, so right. He couldn't explain why, but he knew this was how it should sound and that in a few moments a portal would appear.

Chad faced Amanda in the blackness of the chamber as they sang the required patterns. He was pleasantly surprised to see her ghostly image fade into existence as starlight from outside the newly formed portal reflected off her face. He turned and peered through the gateway at the scene beyond, before he stopped his portion of the chant. Amanda had already quit singing and pushed past him. Moments later they stood in the wet grass and looked back at the impenetrable black disk.

Chad grunted. "No wonder it looked so wrong in Thrush's sitting room. There was only blackness on the opposite side. Standing in there and looking out, you could see a view of the countryside."

Amanda didn't respond. She turned in circles, surveying the starlit countryside.

Chad asked, "Should we close the portal before someone else stumbles in there and gets stuck, or Thrush follows us out here?"

"No need. I don't see anyone around, besides us, who might accidentally wander in there." Amanda's tone was dry. "And I don't plan on stepping back in. We didn't generate a very strong portal. I'd expect it to disappear any minute."

As if on cue, the portal phased out and back in, then dissolved completely.

"Come on," Amanda said. "I know where we are, mostly. There's a big city over this way and we should be able to find someone to help us."

She charged off in the direction she had pointed, but Chad remained where he stood. Amanda stopped and looked back at him. "What's the problem?"

"I guess I don't trust you, Amanda." Chad said flatly. "First off, I don't buy how you threw us in with Thrush and you so willingly jumped into his trap. Secondly, I don't know anything about this area or that city you are taking us to. We just generated a portal. Can't we generate another one to take us where we want without having to walk so far?"

He couldn't see her expression in the darkness, but as she spoke he heard the ringing echo to her words that made him feel ill at ease.

"We can't generate a portal, just you and me, out here. Before, we had the energy of the dimensional chamber to call on. Generating a portal takes a lot of energy. That's why you usually need three people. The chamber itself more or less became our third person."

What she said sounded reasonable, yet there was still a disconcerting ring to her words.

She continued, "I'll be straight with you about the city. It's Sirrus, the capital city of the Cloudside. I know, it sounds bad, but really, there are a lot of people from our side there, and we should be able to contact someone to help us get back to headquarters."

Strangely, there was no negative ring to these.

"You've got two choices. You can trust me or else go it on your own," Amanda said with finality. "I didn't choose to exit in this dimension. But now we're here, we will have to make the best of it, and our best bet is through the city."

Again, no negative ring.

With Amanda apparently speaking truthfully, he might as well follow her lead. He reached for his backpack at his feet, before he realized it wasn't there.

"My backpack," he said with anguish.

"Where is it?" Amanda asked, looking around their feet.

"Right where I left it," Chad snapped. "Back in Thrush's living room. Man, if you hadn't been in such a rush to jump into the portal, we could have thought about what we were doing. Now I've lost my cellphone and the black box."

Amanda sighed and rolled her eyes. "We're not going there again, are we? Can't you let your suspicions go?"

Chad exhaled between pursed lips and shook his head. All his misgivings about her had returned to the forefront of his mind. He wanted to explode, but knew yelling at her would do neither of them any good.

"No, I'm not going there. Let's see what this city is all about."

Amanda headed toward the distant gates. Chad fell in behind her and scuffed his feet along the packed clay path, watching her feet in the dim starlight of the early morning. He pondered as he walked, and hummed.

He thought he only hummed the melody of a song from back home, something he had learned but didn't realize it, until he felt the hairs stand up on his arms and neck. He rubbed at the goose bumps on his forearms and figured it must be colder than he thought. Static electricity snapped and crackled as he ran his hand over his sleeve.

20 - Go Where No Man has Gone Before

Lorantelle watched as Thrush fell backwards into the swirling black portal. The tall man's arms seemed to pinwheel in time with the two-dimensional whirlpool behind him. Shocked disbelief and horror competed for possession of the man's face. A moment before the giant's flailing hand disappeared through the wall of energy, Lorantelle grabbed it and followed him into the icy black miasma.

An instant of overwhelming fatigue washed over the commander as he walked into the dimensional chamber. Fighting the compulsion to sleep, he forced his thoughts to focus on the present predicament. The tiredness eventually abated.

Thrush, however, had fallen victim to his own trap. Lorantelle still held the giant's hand. It hung limp as Brendan Thrush stood, snoring quietly.

"Wake up, Thrush," Lorantelle said and shook the man. It was like shaking a tree. The giant's seven-foot frame felt as if it was cemented to the ground.

"Thrush," the commander barked. He reached his hand up toward where he assumed the other's face would be in the impenetrable black and slapped. A satisfying *thwack* sounded as the flat of his hand met an unconscious sagging jowl. Lorantelle almost wished the man would remain unconscious and he would have a good excuse to hit him again, but Thrush groaned, wavered, and leaned heavily on the commander.

"Come on, you fool," Lorantelle growled and shook him again. "Wake up. Thanks to your arrogant incompetence, we have no idea how much of a head start the fugitives have on us."

"What?" Thrush mumbled groggily as he pushed away from the shorter man.

Lorantelle couldn't see the giant in the dark but felt him snap alert.

"Lorantelle, what have you done? You've trapped us within this portal. The opening is warded from the inside."

"You told me the trap would not hold either you or me. Now it appears to be holding us both. Are you a liar, or just stupid?"

Thrush shuffled around as if searching for an exit. Though the big man struggled and flailed his arms, he never moved a measurable distance from the commander. His voice took on a tone of condescending mockery. "You fool. You've locked us in this dimensional trap. Unless, of course, we have the unlikely fortune that someone wanders into my home uninvited and reaches through the portal to release us before it dissipates."

"Thrush," Lorantelle spat the name like a curse. "For a man purported to be cunning and savvy, your ability to think creatively is crippled by your all-consuming arrogance. Consider it. Your alleged prisoners are no longer in this so-called inescapable dimension, if they were ever here at all."

Lorantelle wiped away the accumulated frustration from his brow with one hand and shook his long black hair from his face. "Do you believe someone came into your home and released your prisoners while you were brewing your tea?"

"No. Of course not," Thrush said. "That would be imposs—"

Lorantelle cut him off, "Then they must have let themselves out by some other way."

"That would be impossible," Thrush said again, but there was doubt in his words this time.

"Stop being moronic and help me find the exit your prisoners used to escape."

"There is no exit." Thrush sounded thoughtful, as if considering his own words. "This dimensional chamber folds back on itself. To walk further in would instantly return oneself to this very same spot."

"How long are you going to keep up this argument?" Lorantelle muttered, running his hand through his hair. He shook his head in frustration. "By your own description, we would be standing right on top of them, if they were here. They've left. Let's find how by re-summoning their portal."

"Re-summoning?" Thrush said thoughtfully again.

"You're not starting the 'repeat what Lorantelle says' game again are you?" the commander asked, but the question was rhetorical, and he continued before the man could reply. "Yes, re-summoning. There is only one way out of a dimension, this dimension, any dimension.

And that is through a portal. *Any* portal can be recalled within several hours of its original casting. There should be plenty of residual energy we can tap into, to bring up a gate that will take us where your prisoners went."

"There is no way," Thrush said, the familiar arrogant confidence returning to his voice. "Those two came to me because they couldn't generate a portal on their own. They couldn't have made a gate out. They would have to possess skills far greater than even mine, to make a portal out of here."

"Yours?" Lorantelle laughed sardonically. "Just humor me. Regenerating a portal is far easier than generating one. Much of the energy of the original portal remains close by, though in a disorganized state. I think even you should be able to do that."

Thrush said nothing and Lorantelle imagined the big man towering above him, just a foot away, cutting through him with an angry glare.

"Good," Lorantelle said. "You start the chant and tap me on the shoulder when you want me to begin the counter melody."

Thrush began the intricate melody with its mechanical and formulaic tonal progressions. Almost immediately, a blinding, swirling opalescence congealed out of the darkness. Unaccustomed as they had become to any light, the brightness was dazzling and they both raised their hands to their faces and shied away.

No sooner had Lorantelle begun the counter melodies than the swirling brilliance snapped into focus and both men looked out upon the breaking of a new day. A fertile countryside spread out in all directions. In the distance, a city perched on an elongated hill.

"So, what was it you said?" Lorantelle asked with heavy sarcasm. "They would need powers even greater than yours to make a portal out? Looks like they made pretty light work of it to me."

He gave Thrush a moment to think and asked, "So, who do you think these two kids are? Just some random teenagers trying to find a missing friend? Or do you think maybe they're a couple of very powerful players in our impending dimensional conflict? And you allowed them to slip through your incompetent fingers."

The commander stepped through the portal onto a dirt road and turned to face the lanky skeleton of a man. Thrush only gazed past him at the orange of approaching sunrise.

"You can stay in there if you wish," Lorantelle said, turning up the road. "I'm getting along before those kids gain any more distance on us."

He didn't look to see if Thrush followed, but soon heard the big man's feet scuff against the packed clay of the road as he hurried out of the dimensional chamber.

"Now, commander," Thrush droned, sounding as if they still sat at his kitchen table, drinking tea and playing word games. "What is your grand plan for returning us to civilization?"

"I have no plan for *us*, Thrush," Lorantelle said as he surveyed the countryside. A sliver of sun peeked above the broadly undulating eastern horizon. "You may go where you wish. I have the fugitives to follow."

"What?" Thrush spluttered. He shook his head and grasped Lorantelle's shoulder with the fingers of one long, skeletal hand. "You brought me to this backwater dimension when you forced me through the dimensional chamber. You have an obligation to restore me to the safety of my abode."

The rising sun turned the giant's sallow features orange. Lorantelle shook his head. "I owe you nothing. Because of your incompetence I am at least a half day behind the two you have let slip through your fumbling fingers."

"Wait," Thrush called, a new note of helplessness in his voice. "Where are you going now?"

Lorantelle sighed and scanned the horizon ahead of them. "Don't you ever get out? Are you so unfamiliar with everything outside your isolated cottage you don't know where we are?"

"My attentions have always been focused on the political needs of our society," Thrush confessed conversationally. "I have never seen the need to travel, nor to study the geography of our dimensions."

Lorantelle jerked his thumb over his shoulder. "Right over there is the capitol city of our world, the Cloudside city of Sirrus. More people live there than in all the rest of the dimensions combined." He turned and pointed at the ground. "And there are the tracks of the two you lost, the Star Daughter's Champion and another unknown factor, cutting through the morning dew to lose themselves in that teeming mass of humanity."

Lorantelle charged off again, and said, "Go where you want. In Sirrus you may find a way back to your safe, pitiful little cottage. But if you want to redeem yourself from your many blunders of the last day, you can come with me and at the very least give me a better description of the two we follow."

#

Thrush spent the next few hundred yards trying to describe the Champion and his companion, though his descriptions of the youths were painfully vague. He did share the girl's name—Amanda Saint Joseph—as he continued speaking.

"It was her own family who alerted me the girl might be arriving with the boy and the two should be detained until called for."

From the corner of his eye, Lorantelle saw Thrush look at him as if expecting a comment—some expression of gratitude. The commander kept his eyes on the road and refused to give the buffoon any satisfaction. Whether the Saint Joseph family had realigned to the Cloudside, or if their confidence in Thrush was a blunder on their part, he would know in time. For now, the answer was not vital. "And the boy?"

"The boy," Thrush repeated thoughtfully. Apparently, repetition was not only an annoying game he played, but his actual manner. "She called him by name. Now, what was it?"

They walked in silence for a time.

"Charles," Thrush said suddenly, yet the name hung there like a question. "She called him Charles."

"You think she was lying?" Lorantelle asked.

"Yes," the big man said eventually, "I don't believe that was his real name. Something in the way she spoke."

"And what did this Charles look like?" Lorantelle asked.

"He was a boy," Thrush said dismissively. "They all look the same. Short hair, dark blond or maybe brown. Skinny, younger than the girl. Maybe eight or ten years old. Always looking at his shoes. He never really looked up."

"Thrush," Lorantelle said with contempt. "You are a veritable fount of information."

21 - A Meeting of Minds

"Enter," Lord Caltone barked when he heard Felipe tap on the door to his private chambers.

The boy approached the desk and bowed. "Your highness, I am here to serve."

"Stand," Caltone growled. "Where is the girl?"

"She's in her room, my lord," Felipe said, clearly confused.

Caltone's anger rose with each inhalation. "Derrick should have informed you to bring her here. Do so now."

"Yes, your highness," Felipe gasped, already halfway to the door.

Caltone watched the messenger leave and pondered how he would punish the boy for his failure. And Derrick. He could not be allowed to believe that giving Felipe only half of the message he was sent to deliver would be overlooked. Caltone grew weary of suffering the incompetence of his faithful commanders' sons. True, it would be a misuse of resources to have their parents here to do the tasks Caltone entrusted to their children. A bit of punishment would help these youths develop greater discipline. Perhaps if he punished their parents, a little discipline would filter down to the children. Caltone smiled and nodded his head.

Just then the knock came again at his door.

"Enter," Caltone all but shouted.

Felipe directed the girl to stand in the center of the room.

"Bow," Caltone heard the boy whisper desperately as he pushed lightly on her back.

Amy shook him off.

"I'll not bow to pigs." She spat the words directly at the supreme leader of the Cloudside, her face defiant.

She wore an old fashioned black velvet dress that reached to the floor. Its only ornamentations were silver buttons at the wrists of the long, closely fitted sleeves, and a narrow black satin ribbon that tied in a bow just below her breasts which gave the dress a high waist. Her hair, held by a ribbon matching the one in her bodice, was clean and neatly brushed. The lady-in-waiting Felipe found had obviously been busy.

"There is no need to be offensive, my lady," Caltone said with a patronizing smile. "I've invited you here to talk. To see if we can't come to an agreement that will benefit both of us."

"The only way you can benefit our people is to withdraw your interference from our dimensions and allow us to pursue our interests in peace."

"That's it, is it?" Caltone's voice snapped with sarcasm. "We leave your people alone to pursue their interests, and we benefit how?" He didn't wait for her to reply. "We won't," he said. "Because your meddling, self-righteous proponents will continue to infiltrate our lands and our people, to sew discord and insurrection. No. Your hypocritical standards will not allow us the freedom from your ideologies you claim to want from ours."

The girl opened her mouth to speak, but Caltone cut her off. "Enough. We must look to the future to find a satisfactory peace for all our people, not dwell on our differences of the past."

Amy began to speak again, but Caltone waved his hand. "No, no, no," he said as he shook his head. "I'm giving you one chance to join with me willingly. The two of us, if we combine our abilities, can subjugate all the people of the dimensions, and bring peace."

"I will never be the force behind subjugation," Amy said through gritted teeth. She folded her arms across her chest. "All people have the right to choose their own path and build their own lives."

"Yet you would choose for them now?" Caltone said like a magician who has set up his audience for a card trick.

Amy didn't answer. She only looked at him suspiciously.

"Join with me and there will be peace." He stood but remained behind his desk. "Under my direction, of course." He leaned on his desk and peered over it at her. "If you choose not to join with me, then you choose war, destruction and death for your people. Where is the freedom of choice in that? Would they choose the suffering your thoughtless, self-absorbed decision would level upon them?" Caltone sat back down. "You don't think of them. You think only of yourself."

"And who will begin this war?" Amy asked, her own voice dripping with contempt. "Who will level this destruction? You. You can't place the blame of your quest for domination on any decision I make."

Caltone considered the girl, his eyes narrowed. A crooked smile raised the corner of his mouth.

Amy took a quick breath and spoke again. "Besides, I know the will of our people. I have been in council with our leaders and they will not accept your unlawful domination. We will fight you to our last man, as the need may be."

His highness laughed quietly—a staccato grunting. "Won't they be surprised when you take that decision out of their hands?"

Amy looked startled but didn't speak.

"As I said, you had one chance to agree willingly to assist me. You've lost that chance." All humor vanished from his voice. He stood and said, "Detail, take your places."

From a side chamber at Caltone's right hand, two men and a woman in long overcoats walked into the room, circled around behind Amy, and took positions an equal distance from each other and their leader. They formed a diamond, with Amy at its center.

"I could do this on my own," Caltone said casually. "But why take even a small risk you might escape, when I have so many who are willing to help me?"

Caltone began the melody and was joined sequentially by the others positioned around the girl. As the volume of their chant increased, Amy stood taller as if she thought her resolve would protect her from the influence of the energy being altered around her.

"I'm not afraid of you."

"Are you not?" Caltone laughed. With increased intensity, he asked, "How about now?"

Amy shook violently, the silver clip slipping from her hair. She coughed. "No. I'm not afraid of you."

Caltone motioned with his hand and his three assistants increased the volume of their intonations. "And now?"

"Your skills of coercion can have no effect on me," Amy said, though her voice became breathy and weaker with each word she spoke. "I am a diplomat, and as such my will is impervious to the effects of those like you and your stooges."

"Your will may be impervious to my influence." Caltone laughed. "It will do you no good if you cannot access it. When a person's soul is separated from their body, the person dies. If the soul is sealed off from the individual's access, are they not likewise dead? The animated dead?"

Caltone laughed again. "It sounds apocalyptic, doesn't it? Your soul is asleep though your body stands and walks and speaks. And who manages the strings of this marionette?"

She glared at Caltone but swayed where she stood, then blinked her eyes and licked her lips.

"You can block my soul, but you can't control it," Amy panted and mopped at her suddenly sweaty brow with the back of one sleeve.

"You can't," she said again, even as her eyes fluttered shut and she slumped to the floor.

The three assistants continued their melody and variations while Caltone stepped from behind his desk and walked to the crumpled form of the girl sprawled across the antique oriental carpet. He nudged her prone form with the toe of his shoe, then motioned to Felipe who had remained by the door. "Get your assistant and take the girl back to her chamber. I will call for her later."

Felipe hurried out of the room as Caltone returned to his chair behind the desk.

"Thank you, gentlemen, my lady. You may leave." Each bowed slightly and left the room through the same door they had used to enter.

He stared at the unconscious girl on his floor. Her only movement was the occasional shallow breath that shifted her shoulders.

"I should kill you now," Caltone said thoughtfully. Then with more resolve he said again, "I should kill you now and be done with you." He clenched his teeth and growled, "But I need you. Only you can unite our disparate sides and hold them while I take control. For now, I will just have to savor the knowledge that the time is coming when I will be able to dispose of you as I wish."

Caltone's reverie was dashed as Felipe burst into the room with a chubby girl, a few years his elder, stumbling along in his wake.

"Felipe, you dolt," Caltone barked. "Have you forgotten how to knock? Have you forgotten all propriety?"

"But, my lord," Felipe stammered. "A hurry... I thought... quickly..."

The boy was clearly distraught and crumbling into greater incoherence by the moment.

"Enough. Take the girl and get out of my sight."

"Yes, my lord." Felipe rushed to Amy's side while motioning the other girl to follow. He lifted Amy by her shoulders while his assistant scooped up her feet. Together the two youths slid the unconscious girl from the room.

Caltone sat back, folded his arms and shook his head.

#

"Come on, Marie," Felipe said as he looked frantically back and forth between their destination, just a few meters away, and his highness's chambers. "We only have to go a bit farther and then we can rest."

"Alright," Marie said and took a firmer hold of Amy's ankles.

They heaved Amy's limp body through the door of the small chamber and up onto the bed then stepped back with a shared sigh. Felipe studied the girl sprawled on the thick down comforter like a cast-off doll. A lock of her hair had strayed from its tie and draped across her face. He reached toward it, but inches from her face, his hand stopped.

He remained motionless.

Standing at Felipe's elbow Marie glanced back and forth between the boy's hand and his face. He stood in a daze, transfixed.

"Felipe," Marie asked, "Are you okay? What is it?"

Felipe shook himself as if waking from a dream.

"Her hair, Marie." His voice was breathy and faint. "It's a mess. Please brush it."

After saying these words, he sighed deeply and lowered his hand back to his side.

22 - Uncovered

Chad looked up through a crack in the floorboards. If he put his eye close to the crack he could see a good portion of the kitchen above the basement where they hid. The amount of sunlight glinting through the window had decreased substantially since that morning when he had first peered through the boards.

"Was this place built by dwarves?" he asked Amanda, who sat on a large cushion in the corner next to shelves built from the same broad rough boards as the floor above them. Jars of preserves and cotton sacks of flour crowded the walls from floor to low ceiling.

"It's a cellar," she said. "Don't they have cellars where you come from?"

"We call them basements, and actually, no, we don't." Chad tried to match her disparaging tone. "The water table is too high. Any basement in my neighborhood would fill up with water in no time."

He crouched as he walked back to where she sat, stooping further to keep from hitting his head on the thick cross beams. He flopped onto the cushion next to her. As he sat, the sound of tinkling bells began again and he had a sudden urge to put his arm around her.

He slapped his face lightly, surprising Amanda who startled with a pretty gasp.

The bells faded, and Chad leaned across her feet to twist the key on an oil lamp set next to her knee. Its circle of dim light expanded out another foot as the flame stretched higher. "We've been in here for hours. Who, or what, are we waiting for?"

"Remember that guy we talked with at the grocery store, just after we got into the city?"

"The guy with all the freckles?"

"Yeah." Amanda "He's a cousin of mine. He's on our side and he'll start a message chain to bring us some help."

"You have more cousins than anybody I've ever met," Chad mumbled, but listened carefully to her words for a high-pitched, ringing overtone. He heard nothing that caused him to doubt her honesty.

"You hardly spoke to him," Chad said with a frown. "How would he know to start that kind of chain? And how will they know to look for us here?"

"Actually," Amanda said, "I didn't need to say anything to him. The fact that we are here in this city is reason enough for him to start the chain that will contact headquarters. Tomorrow we'll move to another location where we should be able to get instructions from the council."

Again, no overtone.

"Why don't we just get a few people together and generate a portal out of here," Chad asked. "There should be plenty of people that can help. You said we would need only three."

"And I also told you before, generating a portal requires a lot of energy," she said with some asperity. "Moving that much energy around creates a lot of noise. Not just the noise we make with our voices to call the portal into existence. Most people with any ability to manipulate energy can hear when a portal is created. There are even some who can follow the sound of a portal to its source."

"Are you saying that if we call a portal, we'll call unwanted attention to ourselves?" Chad asked.

"Exactly. Just be patient and tomorrow morning we should be able to meet up with someone from headquarters who can get us back to safety."

"Is that where we want to go, to headquarters? I need to find Amy and get *her* to safety. I'm sure Derrick didn't take her to Starside HQ."

"I'm sure he didn't either." Amanda laughed. "But unless you have some special people-locating power you haven't mentioned before, the people who may be able to help us find Amy will be at headquarters."

Chad listened to her words which were, again, absent of any hint of deception. He began to doubt he had ever heard anything to indicate she was being deceitful. Still, just to be safe, he remained skeptical about most things she told him.

Chad heard a door open and close above, toward the front of the house. He thought nothing of it at first—the woman who had graciously allowed them to hide downstairs had come and gone often in the previous few hours. Then his ears began to ring with a rapid increase of pressure in his head. Feet scraped the floorboards as people walked heavily into the kitchen.

Chad jumped to his feet, surprising Amanda from a semi-conscious doze. All his feelings of doubt returned in a rush. "We're trapped," he hissed.

"Quiet," Amanda mouthed back. She waved her hands at him as if the motion would silence him while she slipped off the pillow and crawled toward him on her knees.

"It doesn't matter," Chad said with resignation. "They know we're down here, and there's no way out."

"The boy is right," a man's voice agreed from above them. The trap door at the top of the stone steps jerked open. "There is no way out."

The man pulled the door until it flipped over and slammed against the floor. Dust sprinkled down from the boards above their heads, creating a sparkling shower in the rays of light slanting into the basement.

The ringing pressure in Chad's head increased until his eyes throbbed painfully. Shimmering darkness edged into his vision and he worried he would lose consciousness. Gritting his teeth, he mentally pushed back the pressure until his mind cleared enough to be aware of his surroundings again.

The man at the top of the steps said, "It will go better for you if you come up of your own accord. There is no other way out, and I will be irritated if I have to come down and retrieve you." Familiar background noises faded in and out with the man's voice, as if Chad had covered and uncovered his ears while he spoke. What the man said rang true.

"Come on," Chad said and reached down to help Amanda to her feet. Hunched over, they crept to the stairs and looked up at the man who stared down at them with his arms folded across his chest. Thrush stood behind him in a similar pose, but with his right hand on his chin, his thumb and fingers periodically squeezing his cheeks and pursing out his lips.

"That's Lorantelle," Amanda whispered behind Chad as he took the lead up the steps. Chad glared at the man as they reached the kitchen.

Lorantelle said, "Sit at the table. I want some information from you before we relocate you to a secure dimension."

Chad dropped into the chair with the best insolent teenager expression he could muster. He slouched down, crossed his arms across his chest and asked, "What makes you think I have anything to say to you?"

Lorantelle stared at the floor as Chad spoke and appeared to ponder something other than Chad's question. After a short pause the commander stepped to the table, sat across from him and said, "I have been known to be quite persuasive."

Chad felt his stomach drop into his shoes as a cold chill ran the length of his spine, though he couldn't figure out why. He had been threatened by the worst bullies at his junior high and learned that most threats were only that and few followed through with action. He raised his eyebrows at the commander but said nothing.

"Don't think you can play with me, boy," Lorantelle said. "You're a foreigner here. You don't belong and you are completely without defense."

Chad heard the jangling overtone which had often warned him Amanda wasn't being truthful, but as he tried to figure out which part of the statement might have been a lie, Lorantelle began to hum.

Chad was suddenly seized with inexplicable and overwhelming dread. He bolted upright in his chair, leaning on the table for support. His stomach turned over and his head spun with nausea.

The moment the anxiety came upon him, Chad sought the safe place in the back of his mind. Once there he pushed out with all the mental strength he could muster, nearly shouting with relief as he felt the pressure release. He panted as physical weakness spread throughout his body, though the fear and nausea had been replaced with anger and indignation.

Chad laughed at the look of shock on the commander's face and saw Thrush take a stumbling step backwards. The sight filled him with confidence. "That's where you're wrong, Mr. Lorantelle. I may not be from the dimensions, but I belong here just as much as you do."

The commander's face morphed from surprise to contemplation.

"Stop!" Chad shouted and raised his hand as if his palm could hold back an attack. And it did. "I can see what you're doing, so don't waste your energy. It won't work anymore."

"What's your name, boy?"

"Chad," he said. "And I'm a Lorantelle like you. I hear you've ruined my family's name. I intend to make it a good one again."

"Don't be stupid. All the Lorantelles are dead," the commander said, though he didn't sound confident. He closed his eyes and tapped his forehead. Without opening his eyes, he asked, quietly, "Who are your parents?"

"Why would I want to tell you that? So you can go torment her? Them?" he quickly corrected and mentally kicked himself for giving away that his mother might be alone.

"What's your mother's name?" It was a command more than a question.

Chad stared back, determined to remain silent.

"Don't play games with me, boy," the commander's face darkened with anger. "Her name is Annette Baker, is it not?"

"Huh?" Chad grunted as if he'd been slugged in the stomach. How could this man know his mother's name?

"Yes." Lorantelle pushed his chair from the table and stood. "I can see it in your face. Let me give you some advice for the future. Don't play poker."

He headed toward the door. With his back toward Chad, he said, "You look like her." He stopped with his hand on the front door and said, "Thrush, keep an eye on these two. Don't allow them to leave, and don't use energy against them. I need to speak with someone."

All three watched Lorantelle leave, but as the door closed behind him Chad jumped to his feet and went to a window. He peered through the colored panes for a few seconds, then went to the door to follow.

"Stop," Thrush droned in his resonant baritone. "Where do you think you're going?"

Chad reached for the door latch. "I'm going to follow him and I don't think you can do anything to stop me. He said not to use energy against me."

With surprising agility, the giant man stepped to where Amanda watched the interchange with interest. Without warning, he hunched over and locked one long arm around her neck. He stood straight and lifted her from the ground. Gasping and gagging, she struggled for breath and clawed ineffectually at Thrush's forearm.

"There are ways that do not require the bending of energy to convince you to remain," Thrush said with a sneer. "You should sit in that chair over there and relax, or this girl may find it difficult to catch her breath."

23 - A Walk Through Town

Still locked in the crook of Thrush's arm, Amanda's face purpled as Chad stepped through the door. He felt slightly guilty leaving her in Thrush's head lock, but he knew the man was bluffing. Thrush dealt in favors and would earn none by killing the daughter of an influential Starside family. Besides, Chad had heard the jangling discord he had grown used to hearing when Amanda was being untruthful.

Turning left, Chad dashed up the cobbled street to follow Lorantelle through the milling mass of people. He glanced back to see if Thrush had followed, but the house was already obscured by the crowds heading up or down the narrow lane.

Pushing his way up the street, Chad eyed the small houses and shops with little or no space between them. Some even shared a common wall, leaving no alleys or other places for Lorantelle to find quick concealment. The commander hadn't been gone for more than a couple of minutes, and unless he was running as well, he shouldn't be far ahead. Luck was on his side and Chad soon caught sight of the commander's back as the crowd parted to allow him to proceed up the lane. Chad slowed to maintain his distance, and followed covertly.

Without warning, Lorantelle stopped, turned, and strode the few long steps to reach Chad and grab a hold of his jacket. He shook the boy, but appeared more frustrated than angry.

"And Thrush proves the vastness of his incompetence once again." His gaze cut through Chad with an analytical glare. Chad could see the frustration in the man's eyes and heard it in the clipped articulation of his words.

Chad wondered what else the arrogant schemer had done to Lorantelle to anger him so completely, but this man was his enemy and probably not ready to sit down and compare notes.

Lorantelle frowned at him. "You have a lot to learn about the use and control of energy. I could hear you baying like a hound dog the moment you stepped onto the street."

He looked back over Chad's head in the direction of the home where Amanda and Chad had hidden and shot rapid glances around at the people flowing past.

Eventually, he took Chad by the arm and dragged him farther up the road. "Keep quiet, don't make eye contact with anyone and, no matter what, keep your thoughts in close."

"My thoughts?" Chad asked.

"Yes," Lorantelle said as he moved the boy along. "You're broadcasting them like you have a megaphone. If you can't control the volume, try thinking about something unimportant, like the stones in the street. Or better yet, keep an eye on one of the prettier girls walking past. Everyone expects loud thoughts like that from a boy your age."

Chad looked at the crowd flowing along in the same direction they headed and noticed a number of attractive girls. There were more people on the street than when they had arrived in the city that morning, and Chad was surprised by the variety of cultures and nationalities present.

Something else seemed to group different people on the street. At first, he couldn't quite put his finger on it. It wasn't a difference in skin tone or general facial features. As he watched more and more people pass by he decided it wasn't a physical difference, but more of a perception. Some of the people were for lack of a better term, blurred. The image left Chad with a negative impression. Maybe because this man, Lorantelle, had such a blur. For others, Chad felt an inexplicable attraction. The last group, the majority of those who passed, had no blurry signature at all, and Chad felt neither a positive nor a negative pull from them.

His eyes fell upon one particularly attractive girl and his thoughts returned to Amanda, whom he had abandoned to Thrush. Those two were probably working together anyway. Guilt mugged him as his thoughts switched to Amy, the girl he was here to protect; the girl he was here to rescue and return to safety. Where was she now? Was she locked in the dark as he had been? Or worse, was she being tortured or abused by those who wished to gain control of her talents?

Chad felt his head snap back as Lorantelle spun him around and spoke through gritted teeth just inches from his nose.

"On second thought," Lorantelle hissed, "maybe you should just think about the stones in the street".

Without giving him a moment to consider the advice, Chad was dragged along the road again. Not releasing his arm, Lorantelle murmured in his ear as they went. "I need to get you to a place where we can shield your thoughts until I can figure out what to do with you. You need to take this seriously, unless you want to drag every Cloudside agent right to us. It was your thoughts that drew us right to the cellar where you were hiding. Anyone who wants to can reach out and pick up the noise you're making without much effort."

The sun sank and street lamps flickered to life along the length of the street. Lorantelle suddenly pulled Chad through a varnished wooden door that groaned on its hinges, and shut it quickly behind them.

"Be silent," the commander said. "Think of nothing. And if you can't do that, think of a solid color. Blue like the sky, or black like night."

Chad chose the blue sky and concentrated on keeping his thoughts only on that color and not on summer afternoons lying on the grass in his front yard and watching clouds.

Lorantelle paced around the small, wood paneled room, inspecting the walls and flooring as he moved. After a few laps, he stopped behind one of the few chairs at the low wooden table centered in the room. He began a chant Chad had never heard before. Without thought, Chad found the pattern to the melody and joined in after a half a minute. Lorantelle shot him an icy glare but didn't stop his intonations. As they chanted Chad could feel a wall of energy expand out around them. Though it was invisible, he could see it in his mind's eye so clearly, he wanted to reach out and touch it. Within a few moments, the bubble of energy had expanded until it disappeared through the walls of the room.

Lorantelle stopped his chant and within a few notes, Chad did too. He squirmed under the man's withering glare.

"What?" Chad tried to control an embarrassed, anxious grin.

"Why did you do that?" Lorantelle frowned at Chad, then clarified, "Join in with the chant?"

"I don't know," he said. The smile finally won control and spread across his face. "Why? Did I do it wrong?"

"No," Lorantelle said. His face softened to a more thoughtful expression and he sat at the table. "I need to teach you something."

Chad's grin vanished completely as fear gripped him. He leaned on sarcasm for strength and asked, "Teach me a lesson? Like what? How to mind my own business, or keep my mouth shut?"

"No," Lorantelle said with a glimmer of a smile. "While you could truly benefit from both of those, I don't believe you are actually capable of learning them."

He motioned Chad to the seat across from him. "Sit. I want to teach you to control your thoughts and keep them from projecting to everyone within a ten-kilometer radius. If you are to survive an encounter with Lord Caltone, you must master this skill."

"Wait a minute," Chad said warily. "How can I trust you to teach me anything? You could be teaching me to kill myself and I wouldn't even know it. And who is this Caltone guy and what makes you think I will have an *encounter* with him?"

"Caltone is the leader of our, or rather, the Cloudside. I am going to take you to him. You need to do that to rejoin with the Star Daughter. Meeting Lord Caltone is the reason you had to enter the dimensions. The results of that interchange will determine whether you aid or hinder the Star Daughter."

"Why do you think I have anything to do with a Star Daughter, whoever, or whatever that is?"

"Don't be coy. You're her Champion. Anyone who gives you half a glance can see that. Fortunately, I am the only one who knows exactly where you are at the moment." The commander shook his head as if reconsidering. "But, why should you trust me?"

Lorantelle leaned back in his chair and looked at the white plastered ceiling. Chad followed his gaze but saw nothing of interest. "I will tell you openly, boy. In the recent past I have become somewhat disenchanted with the Cloudside objectives. Their fight has never been my fight, but for years I felt isolated and adrift, and found their ambitions gave me a purpose and direction."

Lorantelle tipped his head forward until his chin rested on his chest and he looked down his nose at Chad. "Now, however," the man exhaled a deep sigh, "I find my conscience poking at me and teasing me to make a stand for ideals I had not previously considered worth defending. Especially now, as my son has become involved in the conflict."

He let his words dance on the silence.

Chad looked up at him. "That's me, isn't it? I'm your son."

"Yes." The commander nodded his head slowly.

Chad felt reality drop away and wondered if he was in a dream. The commander sat across the table from him, as real and tangible as anyone Chad had ever met, but such an announcement could only be fantasy. How many times in his life had he wished a man would walk up to him, out of the blue, and say the words, "Chad, I'm your father"? And in his imagination Chad would ask his father why he had left him as a baby. And why had he left his mother to scrape out a living and fend for her small family alone.

But he didn't ask. He couldn't speak at all.

The commander appeared to wait, to allow the revelation to settle for a moment before he sat forward and said, "Now pay attention. We'll have time to discuss the past and its implications later. Right now, you need to learn how to close your mind, to protect yourself, us, as we travel."

Chad rubbed his eyes with the heels of his hands. Lack of sleep was catching up with him. "What do I need to do?"

24 - A Father and Son Chat

"You're not trying anymore," Commander Lorantelle snapped at Chad. "I walked all over your brain that time. You did better when we first started."

"You're right, *Dad*," Chad intentionally laid the sarcasm on thick. "I guess I'm not trying very hard now. It's the middle of the night and I actually keep dropping off."

"When Caltone interrogates you, he won't choose to take a break when you get tired," Lorantelle said with equal cynicism. "You need to be able to maintain your defenses well beyond a few hours into the night."

Chad rolled his eyes. "Do you really believe I'll come across this guy?"

Lorantelle stood and walked around the room, stretching his arms and neck. He stopped when he returned to the space across the table, opposite where Chad sat. When he spoke, the hard edge was gone from his voice. "Yes, I do believe you will come across him. I've already told you, I'm going to take you to him."

Instantly, Chad was awake and alert again, sitting upright on the edge of his hard chair.

"This is a trap, isn't it?" he asked and looked around the room, expecting secret agents to burst out of cupboards and side passages. "You're just softening me up, giving me a false sense of security so you can drag me in and turn me over to him without any kind of fight."

"No," Lorantelle said and sat back down. "Caltone is expecting me to bring you back. He knows you're in the dimensions and that Thrush had you. By now, Thrush has informed him you escaped and is mobilizing agents to find you. If I don't bring you back personally, and soon, any advantage you may be to the Star Daughter will be lost. As it stands, I have the opportunity to hand deliver you to the girl in the place where you will have the greatest opportunity to create havoc."

"Havoc?" Chad asked, hoping for some insight about what he was expected to do.

"Well, you know what I mean," Lorantelle said. "No one knows exactly how you will aid the Star Daughter, but I can't imagine an event like that being anything other than havoc. She may be here to create peace, but it will still come at the price of conflict and with conflict will come chaos and pain."

Chad considered this man, a commander in the Cloudside forces, who claimed to be his father. All his words had rung true, with none of the discordant undertones Chad had heard from Amanda and Thrush. Yet, the blur, the signature around the man, remained. Lorantelle's alignment had to be to the Cloudside.

They stared at one another for a long moment before Chad finally said, "Alright. Let's try again."

"Good," Lorantelle said. "Now, find that safe place in the back of your mind and draw yourself into it."

"Okay," Chad said. "I'm there."

Lorantelle shook his head resignedly. "Yes, you are. You are completely blocked off. Why didn't you do that before?"

"I did," Chad growled. "But I'm tired."

"Get up, then," Lorantelle said and led the way to the door. "We need to get a portal back to the Chateau."

#

Outside, the streets were empty and few of the homes had lights on within.

"We have a ways to walk," the commander said in a hushed voice. "For security reasons, there is only one place in the city where we can transport from and not be attacked when we arrive at Caltone's headquarters. If you keep your voice down, you may ask some of the questions I think you want to ask. Once we're close to the transit department, we'll be under surveillance and it would be best to not appear as anything other than captor and captive."

Chad's mind stalled. He should ask about his father's involvement in his early life, but he wasn't quite ready to know the answers. Instead he said, "Yeah. I have a question. I've noticed something about the people here. Many, such as you, have something like a shadow..."

His voice trailed off. It had hit him as he said the word, where he had seen a similar blur. It was the cat creature, Shadow. When she had phased in and out of her real shape, she had a similar overlaid fuzziness.

He continued, "It's like an overlay of the person, kind of hazy or fuzzy. It matches their body, but seems like it's just slightly out of alignment. I don't know if this is making any sense. A lot of people I've seen in the city have what felt to me like a negative shadow. A few people have a positive shadow. Most people have nothing."

"And I have one of these shadows?" Lorantelle asked.

"Yes," Chad said. "You and Thrush both show a negative shadow. Maybe aura is a good way to describe it, but that sounds like fortune teller stuff to me."

"And you can see this aura?" the commander asked softly.

"Yes, don't you?"

"No." A long moment later, Lorantelle continued, "Many in this dimension, in this city, have the ability or talent to control energy, and serve Lord Caltone. Other talented people serve the Starside. However, most people here, and throughout the dimensions, are just normal people without the ability to control energy. They're trying to live normal lives within the constraints of the alignment in their particular dimension. If they want to leave and go to a differently aligned dimension, they have to find someone willing to make a portal. Right now, in the Cloudside, you have to get permission to make a portal, so it's not easy to leave. Until recently, living in the Cloudside wasn't so bad, if you just did what you were told."

They walked in silence for a hundred yards before Lorantelle said, "I imagine what your seeing is a visual representation of those who are talented as well as their alignment."

A cold chill ran up Chad's back.

"Okay," he said too loudly. And suddenly the frustration accumulated from years of feeling abandoned by a parent pushed out of him. He sought the calm place in the back of his head and stayed there for a moment as he gathered himself.

"Well done," Lorantelle said, sounding impressed.

Chad said more quietly, "Why did you leave?"

"Indeed," Lorantelle said as they walked slowly through the cobbled streets lit only by intermittent gas lamps perched atop ornate wrought iron poles high above their heads. "I have asked myself the same question many times. When I met your mother, your brother had just been born."

Chad glanced quickly at his father's face, though the commander continued to look forward as he spoke, his expression unreadable in the darkness.

"That's right, Chad. He's not my son," Lorantelle continued. "Annette was very bitter about Mike's father's betrayal. She never even told me his name or the circumstances of their relationship. But, the one thing she promised was she would never have more children. Since then I've realized it was the frustration of raising a newborn alone that was speaking at the time.

"We lived happily and quietly for a few years and were eventually married though she never took on my assumed name of Lawrence. You see, Chad, I knew my family history and what our role in the pending revolution would be. I didn't want to complicate that by adding any more Lorantelles to the mix."

The commander's voice broke and he was quiet for a long time. Chad thought about reaching into his father's mind to see what internal battles he was fighting but held back. He didn't want to interfere in what was private. Also, he figured Lorantelle would have much stronger mental blocks set up than Chad could hope to penetrate.

"Caltone knew the formulas," Lorantelle began again, his voice having returned to its usual cold, matter-of-fact tone. "He knew a Lorantelle was required to play an important part when things came to a head. So, one by one he had our family eliminated."

"Mrs. Walker, my English teacher, said her husband was a Lorantelle," Chad said. "He died unexpectedly."

"The florist?" Lorantelle grunted. "Yeah, he was doing more than just making corsages. Caltone couldn't allow him to be the last one of us standing. He only left me alone because he thought I was weak and figured he could control me in the end."

"So, when did you turn to his side?" Chad asked.

"When I found out Annette had become pregnant," Lorantelle said with a tone that could have been either defensiveness or anger. "I realized there would be another Lorantelle. I didn't want your mother, or you, to become another sacrificial pawn in Caltone's game, so eventually I decided the best protection for you would be for me to disappear without a trace. It took time and it wasn't easy but I made my way back into the dimensions, and eventually secured a low-level position in Caltone's organization. He soon realized I was there."

Lorantelle stopped walking and motioned for Chad to do the same. A village square spread out before them complete with a fountain at the center of the patterned brick plaza. He looked at each of the dark shops and spoke quickly and quietly. "It was in his employ that I discovered the extent of my skill. Caltone was more than happy to put my talents to use. He saw what I could do, but I don't think he knows exactly how I encouraged people to talk. My primary ability—to create a sense of dread in people—is actually very similar to what he does. Where mine is a universal sense of doom, Caltone generates a deep fear of himself in the people he touches."

Chad shook his head. "If I know the fear I'm feeling is created by Caltone, can't I just remind myself he is the source of it and then ignore the fear?"

"No. I don't know anyone who has been able to do that. The fear is very real and comes from within you. It's very hard to separate that when it's upon you. It's best to stay out of its reach in the safe place in your head."

Lorantelle motioned again to Chad. "Come on. We're close to the transfer area. Stay in front of me and one step to the right. Don't talk. You're a prisoner now and you need to act like it. Do exactly what I tell you. Look straight ahead, and whatever you do, keep your thoughts inside your own head."

They crossed the plaza to the right of the fountain and headed for the street directly opposite where they entered the market square. A hundred yards away, lights flickered off polished buckles and buttons as guards paced about in the cobbled courtyard of the transfer point.

25 - Forethoughts and Afterthoughts

"Detail, attention," a uniformed man shouted as he saw Commander Lorantelle enter the room, a pace behind Chad and to the left.

"Stop, boy," Lorantelle said, and then to the soldiers, "Carry on."

He strode toward the highest ranked enlisted man. Over his shoulder, he said to Chad, "Stay where you are. You've experienced but a fraction of the pain you'll feel if you try to do something courageous right now."

Chad stood with his eyes directed at the floor. His hands hung limply at his sides as he centered himself in the safe spot in the back of his head. Drawing back his awareness and clamping down his thoughts, he took in the activities going on around him. Each of the soldiers, four men and two women, wore emblems of rank on their lapels, though what they indicated, Chad had no idea. The commander spoke with a man who sat at a table and must have been the person in charge. Two others casually walked to the door through which Chad and Lorantelle had entered. The soldiers stood side by side with their backs to it, preventing anyone from entering or exiting.

"Commander," the man said. "We'd become concerned about your absence. Mr. Thrush and his companion came through hours ago and said you would be along shortly. He recommended we hold you here until an appropriate escort arrives to take you to the Chateau."

"That meddling moron doesn't have the authority to recommend how you eat your eggs for breakfast, while I can order you to spend your next two weeks of leave sitting by yourself in the brig," Lorantelle growled and turned to the door beyond the officer sitting at his desk. The two door guards shuffled their feet at his approach. "Have your detail summon a portal to headquarters immediately. I'll wait with the boy in the courtyard."

He turned to Chad and motioned toward a door. "Come, boy."

The soldiers stepped aside, allowing the two to pass when Lorantelle cut them an icy glare.

Either it was coincidence, or the detail was extremely efficient, Chad couldn't tell which, but as they stepped through the door to the back courtyard, a portal burst into existence at the base of the short stairway. Though the courtyard remained dark, morning sunshine slanted across an expansive grass lawn.

Lorantelle didn't hesitate. He took Chad by the arm and stepped through.

At the Chateau, three men appeared from behind the portal, the tails of their long brown overcoats flapping around their legs as they strode forward and nodded a greeting to the commander. Their stern expressions filled Chad with uneasy foreboding as they silently directed Lorantelle toward the Chateau. Two men escorted Chad while the third walked with Lorantelle across the large lawn to the mansion.

On the porch, outside the entrance to the chateau, Thrush sat at one of many white, wrought iron tables. Though each of the tables was adorned with bottles of wine and goblets, the lanky man appeared to be drinking tea. He raised his cup to them in salute as they passed by him.

They passed through heavy oak double doors and entered the modern reception room where a stern woman sat at a large glass desk. She said nothing, but her out-of-phase aura spun rapidly around her like a whirlwind crossing a dusty plain. The blank expression on her face did little to hide the vindictive grin her aura exuded. Her piercing eyes were aimed not at Chad but at the commander and though she never looked directly at them, Chad could feel her following them as they passed her and entered a passage at the opposite end of the room.

His escort deposited Chad in a small, wood-paneled room while Lorantelle continued down the long hallway. The guards remained silent and closed the door behind him as soon as Chad stepped across the threshold.

Two comfortably upholstered chairs faced each other across a small, round mahogany table with a lamp in its center. The stylized leaded glass lamp shade gave it the appearance of a tiny weeping willow and cast a green and yellow tint over the room...

Chad jerked from a sound sleep as the door to the room swung open and slammed against the wall. Surprised and disoriented by the strange surroundings he struggled to remember where he was and why he was there. A tall, slender boy stepped in front of him and sneered, his long black hair a sharp contrast to his pale skin.

"Did you bring my game player?" Derrick laughed.

Chad's first thought was to ask where Amy was, or demand to see her, but rather than giving Derrick the satisfaction of saying something stupid, he just sat and stared back at the older boy.

You just going to sit there? Chad heard in his mind.

"Are you just going to sit there?" Derrick asked aloud.

Chad looked up at the boy towering above him and almost laughed. He checked to make sure he was still in his mental safe spot and not transmitting his own thoughts before he said, "No. As soon as you leave, I'm going to look for Amy."

She's down the hall, two rooms to the right. Chad heard the words like a stuttering whisper inside his head.

"No one's letting you out of this room," Derrick said, then added with a small, knowing smile, "not until Caltone's done with you. And then you won't be good for much."

Chad used to be so afraid of Derrick. But now, after everything he'd experienced since coming to this fantasy world, Derrick's threats seemed empty and flat, almost disappointing.

"What about Amanda?" Chad asked.

He could see it on Derrick's face, and the voice in his head only confirmed what the other boy was thinking.

She is so hot, the crackling inner voice said.

Chad didn't wait for a verbal repetition, and asked, "Has she joined up with your side?

How'd this idiot know that? the voice said, and Chad rolled his eyes when Derrick tried to play dumb. "What do you mean? Who's Amanda?"

"Never mind." Disappointed he had been right about her, yet encouraged Derrick seemed to be such an easy source for information, he asked, "So, what's this about Caltone questioning me? I thought that Lorantelle guy was some kind of grand inquisitor."

Derrick's face darkened. "What do you know about Lorantelle?"

"Oh," Chad acted thoughtful. "I just heard he ruined his family name by torturing people, getting them to talk about stuff."

Yeah, but he went soft, the wimp, the Derrick voice said in Chad's head.

"He was," Derrick said. "The prophecy says that a Lorantelle will be a pivotal piece in the coming change. But he blew it and Lord Caltone removed him from authority. The rumor mill says there's another Lorantelle now and his highness is going to use that one to get the control he wants."

Someone pounded on the door and growled, "Hey, dog. Bring the boy."

Chad saw Derrick's face flush and heard the voice in his mind, *You're the dog, moron, and you're going to pay for that.*

Derrick looked at Chad and snapped, "What are you laughing at?"

Chad jumped up and to the side as Derrick's out-of-phase shadow leapt at him, then watched the taller boy swing at air when his tangible body followed what the fuzzy signature had predicted.

What the—? the mental voice broke off.

"Come on, Derrick," Chad said, doing his best to keep any contempt from his voice. "You don't want anyone getting mad at you."

He dodged another blow by opening the door and stepping into the hall as the phase signature projected Derrick's next move. The guard in the passage looked as surprised to see Chad leading the way from the chamber as Derrick looked to see him go.

"Come on, dog." Chad flashed a smile at the guard, acknowledging the man's nickname for Derrick.

The guard laughed, and Chad thought he heard a mental *harrumph* from the man as he wiped the grin from his face.

"Escort the prisoner, boy," the guard said. "Or I'll add another negative mark to your record."

Chad let Derrick take him by the arm and push him down the long hallway. As they approached the ornate door to Caltone's chamber, Chad spotted Amanda sitting in the middle of a small bench along one wall. There was enough room on either side of her for both boys to sit on the velvet cushioned bench. She leaned her elbows on her knees and examined patterns in the oriental carpet runner under her feet.

She looked up when Chad hissed, just loud enough for her to hear, "What are you doing here?"

"Be quiet," Derrick said and shook Chad's shoulder, but Chad ignored him.

"Are you here to collect a reward for turning me in?" Chad asked. "Or did you just do it out of loyalty to the Cloudside?"

"I'm not loyal to the Cloudside," she said as she stood. Deep sadness shimmered in her large, dark eyes.

Chad listened closely to her response, surprised to hear her words ring true. In addition, he didn't see any of the signature Cloudside fuzziness to her aura.

Derrick started to move between them, but Chad lifted his hand and pushed it palm out toward the boy and pictured pushing him backwards. He didn't actually make contact, though Derrick still stepped backward, a dazed look on his face.

26 - Playing Games can be a Blast

How—? Chad heard in his mind.

Chad was as surprised as Derrick looked. New skills seemed to be sprouting from him like weeds since coming to the Chateau. If that mental push was an ability that came with being the Star Daughter's Champion, it could come in handy. However, he didn't want Derrick to know it was something he had done and didn't yet know how to control.

"Back off," Chad said between clenched teeth and allowed anger to spice his words. He needed to cover his mental push with a distraction but couldn't think of anything useful. Instead, he glared at Derrick for a moment before turning back to Amanda.

"I'm tired of being pushed around by you people," he said to both at once. Kicking himself for that poor choice of words, He spoke directly to Amanda. "What's that look for?"

"I can't believe you walked out on me," Amanda said, standing up, her hands clenched into fists. Her face flushed red as she spoke and Chad saw tears in her eyes. "Thrush was going to kill me."

"He obviously wasn't going to kill you," Chad said dismissively. "I mean, you're here right now, and you look perfectly alive to me."

The door to Caltone's chambers inched silently open. Chad saw the movement from the corner of his eye and turned to face it directly. A man in a long brown overcoat waited until Derrick noticed him standing in the partially open doorway and gave a small nod before he stepped back into the room.

Both... Chad heard in his mind before Derrick leaned his head through the doorway and asked under his breath, "Both of them?"

He turned back to Chad and Amanda.

"Okay, you two. Come on," Derrick said, and then he smiled menacingly. "You'd better not try to be funny in there or you'll find out how things really work in the dimensions."

It was true enough. Chad didn't know what he was up against. Lorantelle had only told him that Caltone would interrogate him—probably for hours. Whether that would entail only questioning, or include threats, or physical torture, Chad couldn't guess.

He and Amanda stopped in the center of the room in the middle of a rich oriental carpet. Mild fear washed over him like a chilling breeze, though it was mostly blocked by the psychic wall within his mind. Amanda dropped to the floor and cowered, whimpering.

Derrick's muttering inner voice whispered from a step behind them.

Caltone's desk rested on a raised platform so high, they could only see his head over the desk. He leaned forward, his eyes glowing like a cat's at night. "You are the Champion?" His voice was the epitome of ridicule.

Chad checked the boundaries of the safe place in his mind before he dared speak. The walls were up and he felt relatively secure.

"I don't know," Chad said, working the surly teen attitude for all his worth. "No one around here tells me much."

Stupid, Derrick's silent voice said inside Chad's head just before Derrick slapped him.

Chad might have been hit by a baseball from the jarring pain ringing in his ears. His indignation flared and he felt the walls of his safe place waver. Recognizing the danger in allowing Derrick to anger him too much, Chad quickly reined his emotions back in.

"There is no need for violence, Derrick." Caltone's voice was smooth like cream, but Chad watched the other boy pale. "This young man is our guest and we want him to feel comfortable and at home."

Chad was completely out of his league. He was alone in a strange world, dealing with powerful and dangerous people. How could he hope to survive? But then a thought occurred to him. He should be dead already, and yet, here he stood. They needed something from him.

What could that be?

Maybe he should ask.

Still in his mental safe spot, Chad gathered himself. His skin almost tingled from the barely contained energy and he felt his heart jump. "What do you want from me?" His voice was loud and clear. Confident.

"That depends," Caltone was ready with his reply. "Why are you here?"

Chad hesitated. Why was he here? Mr. Snider had said he had to come, and Chad had accepted that declaration so easily, back in Amy's living room. But so much had happened since then. Had his motivation changed? Was he here because he felt guilty for allowing Amy to be taken away, or, more recently, for betraying his dedication to her by throwing himself at her cousin? Was he just being obedient to his friend's father, or was it something completely different?

"I've come to get my friend back," Chad said simply.

"Indeed," Caltone droned from behind the desk. He hadn't moved since he first spoke and was still mostly obscured from view. "I assume you speak of Amy. What is she worth to you?"

"Worth?" Chad said incredulously. "You can't put a value on a person. She's not a possession."

"I'm afraid I will argue with you on that point."
Caltone sat back. In doing so, he disappeared beyond
Chad's line of sight. "This friend of yours is very
valuable to me. I know exactly how much she is worth."

In a twisted way, Chad saw Caltone's logic. Amy
could win him control of the entire dimensional world,
or could cost him his control of the Cloudside.

"What's she worth to you, boy?" Caltone asked again.
His voice rose in pitch and seemed to bounce off the
mahogany paneled walls of the wide chamber. "I could
destroy her in a heartbeat and she would be gone
forever. Or, you could help me win her to our side. Aid
me in my struggle to unite our peoples and you would
not only save her life, but you could then have her all to
yourself. Is her life valuable enough to you, for you to do
this small task for me?"

He was pushing Chad into a logical corner. Before he
could agree to something he would regret, Chad
changed the subject.

"Where's Lorantelle? I thought your lap dog did all
your bullying."

"Yes, Lorantelle," Caltone mused. "I thought he was more than he truly was. He was not what I needed, however. I have replaced him."

Caltone stood and stretched himself to his full height before walking around to the front of the desk where he casually leaned against it.

"Detail," he said.

A side door opened and two men and a woman entered, their long overcoats nearly black in the dim light of the chamber.

"Derrick," Caltone said. "Take the girl back to her room. Her presence is not necessary at the moment but keep her ready. When the time is right, I think she will be a satisfying addition to our proceedings."

Once Derrick dragged Amanda away, the three took their positions around Chad. Caltone began humming. Shortly, the others joined with him.

Chad knew this couldn't be good, being surrounded on four sides by obviously powerful Cloudsiders. He knew they were about to bend energy against him but didn't know to what end. Perhaps they would try to force him to join with Lord Caltone.

Unsure what else to do, Chad found his safe spot, mentally hunkered down and braced for the assault.

A whirlwind of fear brushed lightly against the walls he had constructed as the four people made tentative attacks on his mind. *That's right. Caltone deals in fear,* Chad thought as the intensity of the storm increased. His father had told him he wouldn't be able to tell Caltone's fear from his own once it was inside his head, so Chad reinforced his walls to keep that fear outside his mental shield.

Chad prepared himself for an all-out assault. It never came.

He watched the men before him with interest, unable to see the woman directly behind his back. All showed the stress of intense concentration on their faces, yet Chad continued to feel nothing. Caltone frowned. Chad turned his head and considered the man on his right, and then, just as casually, the man to his left. Nothing breached his defenses. In fact, none of the prodding in his mind ever indicated the four in the room even knew where to find Chad on his safe little island of consciousness. Stray balls of power settled like discarded water balloons around his feet. He wanted to step across his mental boundary and gather the spheres so he could hurl them back at the intruders. Unfortunately, he didn't know if such an action would open him up for assault, or possibly allow these intruders to know he was aware of them.

#

Hours passed. Still safe in his mind Chad looked around the dim room for a chair or other place to sit, and saw next to the door through which he had entered, a small upholstered bench similar to the one in the hallway.

"My legs are getting tired. Do you mind if I sit down?" he asked before turning and stepping toward the bench.

His question was lost in a cataclysm that knocked Chad to the floor. His ears rang, and he coughed at the acrid smell of ozone along with thick white smoke that spread through the room like fog.

Chad climbed back to his feet. Caltone's gaze bored through him with glowing eyes. The ringing in his ears subsided, and he heard Caltone's exclamations.

"What have you done?" The clearly shaken Cloudside leader leaned heavily against his desk, running his long skeletal fingers across the sweaty skin of his bald head.

27 - Goodbyes and Hellos

Still dazed and completely confused, Chad looked around himself, turning in a circle as he took in the damage. The three men in overcoats lay sprawled like neglected dolls in the dissipating smoke. When Chad turned back to face Caltone, the Cloudside leader was seated behind the desk once more. He spoke into an intercom, "Julia, send a containment detail. We have a situation."

The water balloon-sized bubbles of energy previously scattered around his feet had disappeared.

Were they what caused the explosion?

The door to the chamber burst open and several large men rushed in, flooding the room with a melee of emotions—fear, anxiety, anger—but no actual words in his head as when Derrick was near.

Caltone spoke from his desk. "Take the boy back to his room, but be vigilant. He is more powerful than you may think."

The guards eyed the crumpled forms on the floor before approaching Chad warily.

"Don't bother," Chad said, taking advantage of their temerity. "I know the way."

He strode from Caltone's chamber.

As the door closed and locked behind him, Chad was both pleased and concerned to find Commander Lorantelle in his room. He immediately burst into an account of what had just happened, but his father raised his hand, demanding instant silence.

"Listen up," Lorantelle said to his son. "It won't be long before the detail supposedly escorting me out of the Chateau realize I'm gone, and I don't want them to find me in here. They already have orders to kill me as soon as they get me off the grounds. If they know I spoke with you, it will only make it harder for you to do what you need to do."

"They're going to kill you?" Chad gasped, surprised to find how much he cared.

"They'll try," Lorantelle said with a smirk. "There is no time for that. Listen. You must get Amy out of here. Amanda has an extraordinary gift for casting portals.

Use her skills to get Amy to the Starside headquarters. A small nudge from you will amplify her power. As her Champion, you have that ability. The three of you should be able to pop open a portal on the prime minister's front porch."

"I'm sorry," Chad said, and realized how true that was for several reasons. "I don't trust Amanda. She's lied to me from the start. I've known that since the first time I touched her thoughts."

"It's one of the interesting anomalies of the dimensions," Lorantelle said with a thoughtful expression. "Both sides are always present to one degree or another. Every person, no matter how strong they are in their loyalty to their faction, will have at least a little of the other in them. It's why this war will eventually become so fierce. The real battle will go on in each of us."

"I don't have any of the Cloudside in me," Chad said defensively. "I hate the Cloudside. They stole Amy and messed up my whole life."

"Chad," Lorantelle said, kindly. "You're my son. I have much of the Cloudside in me. Whether you know it or not, there is some in you too. Now, Amy, on the other hand. I think she might be the only one who doesn't have anything but Starside. However, that doesn't mean she can't be swayed to assist the Cloudside if she can be convinced it will benefit the majority of people."

The commander scratched his chin thoughtfully. "As far as Amanda goes, her family is deeply involved in politics. I think the negative side you feel from her is coming from how she was raised. Her family is always looking for ways to turn political advantage toward themselves, regardless of how it will impact other people. Still, I think you can trust her."

"What about Caltone?" Chad asked. "Shouldn't we do something about him first?"

"Like what?" Lorantelle asked. "Kill him?"

"Well," Chad hesitated. "We can't just let him continue to abuse people."

"And how do you think you will do that? He is powerful. Also, are you willing to accept the responsibility of killing a man? It's a very personal thing and leaves some heavy baggage behind. Even when it's justified."

Chad thought for a moment. "Maybe I could set off another bomb, like I did in his chamber."

Lorantelle laughed. "That explosion was the result of their own foolishness. They were probably trying so hard to break through your inherent defenses they forgot to set up a safety valve for the back flow of energy. When you stepped out of the way it broke their equilibrium. They blew themselves up. You noticed, I'm sure, that Caltone was relatively unaffected?"

Chad said nothing.

Lorantelle headed for the door. "I need to return to my escort and deal with them appropriately." Reaching for the doorknob, he turned back to Chad.

"I'm proud of you, son," he said and opened the door.

"Dad," Chad said and paused. He'd never said that to anyone before. The word felt awkward and surreal. "Come with us, to the Starside. You can help us cast the portal."

Lorantelle closed the door again and held out his hand. Chad wondered if he was meant to take hold of it, but before he could, the commander asked, "What do you see, Chad? Do you see my aura?"

The familiar out-of-phase signature danced around his father's outstretched hand and arm.

"Yes," he croaked as uncontrolled emotion choked off the word.

"Yes," Lorantelle agreed grimly. "And it doesn't fade quickly, nor will your Starside forgive easily. I have been the cause of a lot of pain to a lot of people. I'm easily recognized, and people won't forget what I've done. They won't believe I've changed."

He opened the door again. "Amanda is across the hallway. Amy is down two doors on the right."

And he was gone.

Chad didn't rush to the door to watch him retreat down the passage like the fugitive he was. Not knowing if he would ever see him again, he wanted to remember his father proud and confident.

#

With a quick glance to the left and right Chad crossed the hallway to Amanda's room. Tapping lightly, he pushed the door open without waiting for an answer.

Seeing him, Amanda sat back in the chair and let out an elongated sigh. Chad closed the door as quietly as he could.

"There's nobody in the hallway," he said. "I wonder where everyone is."

"Is that really what you came to tell me?" she demanded, sounding unsure. "You don't know where anybody is?"

"No. Of course not. It just occurred to me as I crossed the hallway. I mean, there have been people guarding us constantly since we got here. Where have they all gone?"

Amanda just shrugged.

"What I came to say is, we need to get out of here." Chad scowled. "My d— Well, Lorantelle said we need to get Amy to the Starside headquarters as soon as possible. He seemed to think you have a special skill with generating portals, and I might be able to help."

"Why would Lorantelle say that?" Amanda asked, dubiously. "He's one of them. It's probably just another trap."

"No," Chad said firmly. "He's not the guy we thought he was. In fact, he's pretty sure the Cloudside is about to try to kill him."

Maybe they already have, he thought to himself.

"Don't get me wrong," Amanda said. "I'm all for getting out of here, but how are we going to find Amy?"

Chad waved her toward the door. "I know where she is."

28 - What? You Again?

They pushed open the door to Amy's room, which was larger than either of the rooms Chad and Amanda had been in. It even had a bed and an attached bathroom. However, the girl sitting on the bed was not Amy.

Two things about this girl stood out to Chad.

First, she had been crying, and may have been for some time. Her nose and round cheeks were bright red. With her mass of short brown curls and slightly chubby frame, she had the appearance of an adorable, over-large garden gnome.

Second, she had the telltale signature of the Starside. The boy who stood next to her spoke first.

"Who are you?" It was both a question and a challenge as he stood with his feet apart and planted below his stocky frame. He balled his hands into fists at waist level like a fighter waiting for the right opening to throw a punch. This boy, who appeared to be about Amanda's age, had no aura dancing around his body.

Chad stepped forward, feeling sorry for both the girl crying on the bed, and the young man apparently defending her. He stepped forward, held his hand out to the boy. "My name is Chad. Amy is my friend and I've come to take her back home."

Apparently, honesty and directness were the right approach in this situation. A smile lit the other boy's face as tears suddenly filled his eyes, though he fought valiantly to keep them in their place.

"I'm Felipe," he said as he took Chad's hand. "I was Amy's, um, guard."

His face brightened when he turned to his companion, placing an encouraging hand on her shoulder. "And this is Marie. She is my girlfr—" He cleared his throat, "—very good friend. She helped me with Amy."

"They came and took her away." Marie's voice broke as she wiped tears from her cheeks. "She hasn't been herself since Caltone attacked her yesterday. Then they came for her, just a few minutes ago. They didn't even say anything. She just got up and followed them."

"Do you know where they took her?" Chad asked. "I don't care if I have to march right into Caltone's office; I'm going to get her now."

"Chad," Amanda said tentatively. "If she's in Caltone's office, there is no way they're going to let you back in there. And even if you did, how do you think you're going to get her out?"

Chad headed toward the door. "He'll let me in because he wants me there. He wants to destroy me and he wants to do it up close and personal. That's just the way he is. I'll take Amy with me when I leave. He won't be able to stop me."

He yanked open the door. "Come on. Amy will need all of our help."

They headed down the hall in a clump.

As reality slapped him on the back of the head, a sudden wave of self-doubt overwhelmed Chad. Who was he to confront a master power wielder like Caltone? Yet, a sense of confidence simmered beneath his fear. Perhaps it had something to do with his designation as the Star Daughter's Champion.

He glanced at Marie as they hurried along.

"Marie, I know you can manipulate energy, and I can tell Felipe can't. Can you assist Amanda in drawing a portal? If possible, we need to land on the Starside prime minister's doorstep. Lorantelle told me Amy would need to help her with aiming one to the right place, but if she's in a trance or something, she might not be too much help."

"I know the prime minister," Marie admitted, to Felipe's apparent surprise. "I can direct a portal there if Amanda generates it."

"Lorantelle's your dad, isn't he?" Amanda asked as if the clouds had just parted exposing the bright sun above. "That's why he's been sharing so much information."

Marie and Felipe turned toward Chad with a shared expression of astonishment.

"Yeah," Chad said. "I'm not sure how I feel about that either, but it's nothing I can change. And who knows? He could already be dead by now and it won't matter either way."

The comment had come reflexively. Chad couldn't count the number of times he had said something dismissive about his unknown father, out of cynicism or self-defense. Somehow the words felt wrong and disrespectful, now he knew who his father was, and his death was a very real possibility. The loss was worse than anything he had ever felt before.

Outside Caltone's door Chad said to the others, "I need you to wait out here. I don't know how I'm going to get Amy back, but I don't want any of you to become pawns for Caltone to throw against me. Once I have Amy, we'll need to get out of here as fast as we can.

The door was unlocked as Chad assumed it would be, the knob turning easily in his hand. Feigning a confidence he didn't feel, he opened the door and stepped into the dark chamber. The curtains had been pulled back to expose a large picture window to the Cloudside leader's left. The starlight barely illuminated the side of Caltone's face. Incandescent light from lamps set at intervals around the walls of the room gave the leader's large oval head a yellow tint.

Amy stood behind Caltone and to his right, head bowed, eyes unfocused and directed toward the floor. She looked like an antique porcelain doll in her high waisted black dress. Her hands and feet were as pale as bone.

The three of them appeared to be the only ones in the room.

"Where are your dogs?" Chad mocked. "I didn't think they would want to leave their master's side."

"You don't belong here, little boy," Caltone hissed. "I'm giving you an opportunity. Leave unopposed, right now."

"I'm not going to argue with you," Chad said, his voice confident to mask his overwhelming feeling of inadequacy. "And I plan to leave, very soon."

The door behind him opened an inch and then slammed shut. Several dull thumps sounded against the door along with a commotion, then everything was silent except for the sound of blood pounding in Chad's ears.

"Amy," Chad said as firmly as he could without his voice shaking. He saw her flinch, but remained immobile. "Come on, we need to leave."

Caltone hummed a tuneless melody and fear spun around Chad like leaves on a winter breeze. Chad stood securely behind his mental screen, struggling to find a way to use the energy swirling around his feet to lash back at this powerful and experienced leader. Unlike Caltone, he was unfamiliar with the use of power.

Out of ideas, Chad bolted for Amy. He leapt three long steps to where she stood, grabbed her by the hand, and pulled her off the raised dais. Her fingers were cold in his grip.

"Come on," he shouted. "We're leaving."

Caltone's swirling energy whipped into a whirlwind and fear gnawed at the edges of Chad's self-control. They were halfway to the door when Amy dug her heels into the thick carpet and pulled Chad to a stop.

A new energy assaulted his mind. Amy had joined with Caltone and suddenly Chad's overwhelming desire was to do as she wished.

Chad dropped his awareness away from everything else and concentrated on the safe place in his mind. The swirling vortex of Caltone's assault spun around him with a roar like the pounding crush of a waterfall that echoed and vibrated his protective mental walls.

Through it all, Amy's energy was a battering ram against Chad's pitiful brick wall. He wanted to give up, to let his wall crumble, accept Amy into his mind, and do her will.

Her will.

Amy's will didn't match Caltone's. She didn't want to cave in to the Cloudside lord and follow his plan.

He singled out Amy's blasts of energy as they pounded him through Caltone's whirlwind of fear and confusion. Her head bowed, her arms extending straight forward from her shoulders and her fists side by side, her energy pulsed rhythmically against him.

Anticipating her next jolt, Chad caught it and held on. He took the energy from her attack, wrapped it back around her, and snapped it tight.

Caltone's whirlwind whipped faster around the two, tearing at the connection between them, threatening to pull them apart. Chad threw his arms around Amy and locked the fingers of one hand around his wrist, pulling her body to his.

He found the safe place in his mind and pulled Amy in. Though physically locked in his arms, in his mind they stood at arm's length holding hands. Slowly, Amy blinked open her eyes and looked up into Chad's.

When she spoke, her whisper drowned out the hurricane's roar in his physical ears. "You are more powerful than he is. He can't stop you, if you find control."

Something heavy struck Chad's head, jerking him from his safe place and back to reality. Papers, books, and small pieces of furniture spun around the room in the whirlwind. Caltone stalked toward them, inhibited somewhat by the wind of his own creation. Amy's eyes were closed again, though she felt less rigid.

Still wrapped in his arms, he dragged her toward the door. "Give me some help, Amy. We need to get out of here."

Slowly she acquiesced and moved along with him toward the door. Behind them, Caltone screamed.

Use the energy, Amy's words spoke into his mind. *Use his energy.*

Chad saw it then—the energy Caltone used to create the whirlwind. Great eddies of whirling power like gusts of snowflakes propelled the wind and debris around the room. He pictured a stone wall in his mind and threw it up between Caltone and himself, causing the energy to pile up in a great bank, further blocking Caltone's progress.

Amanda, Felipe, and Marie's anxious faces gaped at Chad as he pushed through the door with Amy in tow.

Felipe smiled, his teeth stained red by blood oozing from a split in his lip. His face was red, one eye swollen nearly shut as blood trickled from the corner of his mouth. Chad wanted to ask what had happened but was worried Caltone would be upon them at any moment.

"Quick," Chad gasped, looking back over his shoulder at the door to Caltone's office. "Amanda, Marie, make a portal."

"We can't. Not inside," Marie said and looked at Amanda who nodded her agreement.

"Then let's get out of here." Chad pulled Amy down the hall. Still in her semi-trance, she stumbled and dragged her feet.

When she suddenly seemed to be moving more smoothly, he saw Felipe had supported her under her other arm. The two boys moved her quickly down the straight passage toward the front office and the exit.

The severe woman at the front desk stood as they ran into the entry room. Her scowl deepened as she feebly called out, but she didn't try to stop them as they ran by. Chad considered how no one had resisted them as they ran from Caltone's office. The reason became clear as the four teens slammed open the front door and spilled out onto the landing at the top of the stone steps.

Past the wrought iron tables with empty glasses and discarded wine bottles, across the broad flat lawn, spread evenly around the perimeter along the edge of the low stone wall, more than a hundred over-coated men and women stood ready to attack.

29 - Portals and Waves

Amanda and Marie stumbled to a halt at the bottom of three broad steps. "A portal. Come on. Quick," Chad shouted from above them where he and Felipe supported Amy.

Amanda closed her eyes, dropped her hands down to her sides, and exhaled a deep breath. She began the portal generation song and Marie picked up the melody and joined in after only a few notes. Amy stood between the two boys, limp, her head bowed, her eyes half shut. She swayed to a rhythm neither the singing girls nor the boys standing to either side of her could hear.

As the melody took shape the vague outline of a portal shimmered just a few feet in front of them. Chad recognized the melody. It was similar to the underlying melody of the dimensional chamber where Thrush had trapped them—similar, yet slightly different.

The portal wavered for a moment, then disappeared. Amanda turned. Anxiety and strain etched lines of worry across her forehead. She called to Chad, though he stood just a few feet away, "It's not working with only the two of us. The conflicting energy is overpowering us. We need another voice."

Leaving Amy in Felipe's hands, Chad stepped close behind the two girls. He relaxed his thoughts, taking in the underlying melody. He let its rhythm and chord progressions settle in his mind.

Dizziness overcame him and he shook his head to clear stars spinning past his eyes.

Abruptly he sat on the ground and looked around for his companions. They all appeared to be sitting as he was and were equally as confused. As the clouds cleared from his ringing head he remembered a wave of energy blasting out from the combined Cloudside minions encircling the lawn, and presumably, the rest of the Chateau.

"That was stupid of me," Chad grumbled as he climbed back to his feet. Amanda and Marie stirred but remained where they were.

This time, he was ready when the assault came. Standing in his safe place, eyes and mind wide open, he visualized the shock wave as the Cloudside forces threw it. Transfixed, he held it for an instant. Entirely different than Caltone's whirlwind of fear, an iridescent, roiling wall of energy billowed three meters high along the visible length of the Cloudside assailants. It waited like an angry dog straining against its chain. Then with a roar, the wave crashed forward.

Like the small pulses of energy Amy had thrown at him in Caltone's office, Chad hoped this wave could be held and manipulated. Maybe, if he could bend a small portion of it to his will, he could protect himself and his friends.

As the pounding turbulence approached, Chad threw up a wall of his own as he had against Caltone. The tidal wave never slowed. It absorbed his wall, increasing its height, and pounded forward.

"That didn't work," he muttered. If he couldn't block it, maybe he could thin it out. Instead of trying a higher wall, Chad imagined the wave coming toward him as a gentle, flowing river. Instantly, the rush subsided into a placid pool of energy, lapping at his ankles.

He called the power to him and lifted it above his prostrate companions. In his mind he took it to the very edge of his safe place. With a calm exhalation he blew the energy wave back out at the waiting minions.

They were ready for him, however, and brought up a buffer halfway back to the low brick wall, holding the retreating energy in place as they fired a second wave to combine with the first and push it back with redoubled intensity.

Amanda and Marie scrambled back up the steps to crouch behind Chad with Amy and Felipe.

Initially, Chad worried a doubled blast would be more than he could control. But, having learned to dissipate the energy, he used the distance the wave had to travel across the open field to decelerate it, gather up the energy, and send it back with very little effort. He soon found the exercise of catching and returning the waves as simple as pushing someone on a swing. Still, it was exhilarating to be manipulating energy this way and his mental strength expanded with each repetition.

Chad said between assaults, "Draw the portal, quick. I'll hold them back."

"We need a third," Amanda said.

"Try," Chad begged as he inhaled, held his breath, and blew back another wave. "You did it with just two when we were at Thrush's place. Can't you just try?"

"Thrush led at his place. I don't know how to be primary with only two," Amanda cried, despair straining her words.

Expecting to fend off another energy wave, Chad turned back to the assault, only to find the steady wave had been interrupted, with a large gap knocked out of its center. He surveyed the line to see what had changed. Dozens of the agents in a group directly across the lawn were bent over or thrashing about holding their hands to their heads. Their long brown overcoats flapped about their legs.

Standing behind them on the low stone wall was Commander Lorantelle.

As more agents ran to their compatriots' aid, Lorantelle turned his attention to them. Everyone who approached stopped in their tracks and either fell to the ground or turned and stumbled away. However, the commander eventually reached his limit. For every additional person he took on, one was released and resumed their attack. Horror filled Chad as Lorantelle swayed from side to side, struggling to control the press of agents trying to surround him.

"Dad!" Chad called out, though he knew Lorantelle would be unable to hear him from that distance.

Chad heard in his mind, *Stupid wimp*, just before his head rang while pain exploded inside his skull like an alarm bell. His vision faded to gray and little lights danced before his eyes as he dropped to his knees and fought to remain conscious.

"You don't belong here. You're a loser," Derrick said from behind where Chad crouched on the ground. A wine bottle hung loosely in the pale boy's hand.

"There are a couple of people who disagree with you," Chad grunted over his shoulder, rubbing the back of his head.

"There'll be none left by the end of the day," Derrick said between gritted teeth as he hauled his foot back to kick Chad in the stomach.

The blow never came. Chad looked up in time to see Felipe plant a solid strike from his own wine bottle on the side of Derrick's face. The tall, dark-haired boy stood for a long moment with a dazed look, then collapsed to the ground.

By now, Lorantelle had two dozen of the over-coated combatants cowering at his feet. However, that many more pressed in on him from all sides, attempting to overwhelm him.

The remainder of the Cloudside forces had returned their attention to Chad and resumed their assault.

The waves of energy bore down upon them again, yet Chad could feel something had changed. He still repelled attack after attack, but each successive wave required more effort to return it to the Cloudside. Each breath burned as he dragged the night air into his lungs. His head throbbed and his ears rang each time the rushing, hammering sonic barrage beat upon him. Then a telltale undercurrent of fear joined the Cloudside attack.

"Keep fighting it, boy," Caltone said coolly from the top of the stone steps just a few yards behind the youths. "The more waves you hold off, the more complete your annihilation will be when their combined energy finally breaks through and catches you off guard."

"Let them go, Caltone," Lorantelle said from so close behind Chad, he jumped at the sound."

"*Lord* Caltone," the Cloudside leader corrected dryly, placing special emphasis on the title. His words dripped with hate. "I have to admit, I'm a bit surprised to see you here, and alive. It appears I need to instruct some of my staff on how to carry out my orders."

"You won't need to," Lorantelle said, matching Caltone's air of indifference. "Their incompetence won't be an issue for you any longer."

"Well, then," Caltone said with a contemplative tone. "You've eliminated that problem and made it easier for me to eliminate another. You always were efficient that way." He glanced toward Chad, then back again. "I thought you would be the important player in my end game, commander. But it doesn't matter. The two of you have played your parts."

A wave of energy rushed past Chad like a gust of static-charged wind as Caltone raised his voice and reinforced his troops with a short, melodic chant. Fortified, the minions sent energy rushing toward Chad. He braced himself within the walls of his mind, prepared to take hold of the strike and send it sailing back.

Vague anxiety tickled the back of Chad's thoughts. He spun around to find his father and Caltone locked in a battle of energy.

Before the next wave could hit, Chad seized his opportunity and gathered the scattered energy from around the open grounds, focusing it into two cylinders. He aimed the first around the four youths at the bottom of the stone stairs—the other around his father.

Caltone uttered a quick melodic phrase and the entire chateau shook. Lorantelle barely flinched though chairs and tables toppled sending wine bottles and goblets clattering across the porch to bounce harmlessly off the protective cylinders.

His attention divided between his father's battle and the onslaught from the minions, he miscalculated the speed of its approach. Their energy wave knocked Chad from his feet. He lay on his back trying to clear his head while the roar of battle pitched and rolled. From the corner of his eye he saw the energy cylinders begin to fade leaving his friends in danger from flying debris.

Chad struggled to hands and knees as he gathered latent energy and reinforced the translucent walls.

"I'm stronger than you, Lorantelle," Caltone growled, his face a mask of hate. "You're no match for me. You never have been."

"We appear to be very equally matched," Lorantelle replied dryly.

"True," Caltone began, and then suddenly bent, clutching his stomach. He gasped and straightened back to his full height. "If it was just you and me, we could remain at an impasse for some time. However, I have the combined strength of my followers to call upon as well." Caltone laughed. "You hadn't considered that, had you?"

Actually, I had." Lorantelle winced and wiped sweat from his brow. "Again, we are about even."

"You think these children are an equal match to an entire contingent of my most powerful servants?" The Cloudside lord's voice sounded high and pinched with incredulity.

"No, not really," Lorantelle countered and looked at Chad thoughtfully before he turned back to Caltone. "No. Just the one."

Caltone threw his head back and laughed.

Energy buffeted Chad outside the walls of his safe place and he considered his father's words. His father had faith in him as he cowered on the ground. Chad wouldn't allow that faith to go unfounded and forced himself to stand again.

When the Cloudside leader stopped laughing and turned his gaze directly at Chad, there was no humor in his eyes.

"Very well," Caltone said, barely loud enough for Chad to hear. "You have condemned the boy. His death will be another on your hands."

Caltone raised his hands above his head and called, "My people, leave the others and attack the boy!"

Energy shifted away from Chad as a wave drawing back from the beach and then swelling for its next assault on the sand. As the screaming wall of energy contracted toward him, Chad steeled himself for the impact. He held his arms in front of his body, his hands balled tight as if preparing for a fist fight, his eyes squeezed shut. Seizing hold of the raging maelstrom with his mind, he flung it back toward the attackers, but it quickly slowed to a stop, like a heavy ball rolling across sand.

Chad despaired. He didn't know how much more abuse his body and mind could take.

There was a light touch on his arm.

"Step out, Chad." It was barely a whisper.

"Amy?" Chad's eyes snapped open and he saw her standing next to him.

"Step out and protect me," she said and turned, standing in front of Chad to face the legion of Cloudside power wielders.

Air pressure rapidly climbed as the combined minions gathered another mountainous wave of power to send against them. The behemoth they finally unleashed dwarfed all others and came crashing forward like a freight train. Moments before it collided with them, Chad stepped outside the protective walls of his safe place.

He became one with Amy.

As the Star Daughter's Champion his capacity for power increased a hundred fold and he felt massive, as large as the chateau behind him.

The colossal energy wave collapsed upon them, the combined energy splashed and swirled like water in a pool over a protective dome covering Chad and Amy. He reached out with his mind, gathering the energy around them into an enormous bubble the size of a hot air balloon rising above them. He drew its boundaries in, condensing it smaller until it formed a ball he could hold in his arms. Fear and anxiety, discouragement and futility, roiled about inside the globe—pieces from the battle still raging behind him as well as other emotions and sensations generated from Caltone's subjects.

Chad condensed the ball smaller and smaller, compressing the energy within like a star collapsing in on itself. He held it on the palm of his hand, as heavy as the earth they stood upon, yet as light as balloon. Chad's skin tingled, and his vision began to fade, absorbed by the thrill of control and the rapture of the concentration of power.

With a great shout, Chad cast the concentrated cataclysm to the minions circling Caltone's mansion. It began its arc slowly like a soap bubble rising gently into the sky, but increased in speed, geometrically, until it raced like lightning and struck the center of the over-coated followers. With a blinding flash the ball released its energy scattering many across the manicured lawn. Others collided with the low rock wall and hedges and were left unconscious or groaning in pain.

"No!" Caltone shouted.

"Generate the portal," Chad called to his friends, and turned to his father. Caltone now cowered beneath the commander's gaze.

With Amy's clear voice as primary and Amanda and Marie joining in right after, the air shifted, and a portal began to form.

"Dad," Chad called. "Come with us to the Starside." He motioned toward the gossamer disk which had already bloomed up at the youths' feet.

"I'm sorry, Chad," Lorantelle called with obvious regret. "As I said before, there are many in the dimensions who have not forgotten the part I played.

Nor will they quickly forgive. Go quickly while I still have *his highness* under my thumb. I'll make my own escape."

"Come on, Chad," Felipe called. The others stood at the threshold of the portal and waved toward him impatiently. "We must pass through quickly, before those on the opposite side shut it down."

With a final glance back at his father, Chad took Amy's and Amanda's hands and stepped though into Starside headquarters.

30 - A Hero's Welcome

The world skidded nearly to a halt.

The moment they passed through the portal, Chad and his four companions were blasted to the ground by security forces in the courtyard of Starside headquarters. Latent energy from the attack swirled around their feet and splashed against the brick walls of the enclosed area.

"What are you doing?" Chad screamed as he leapt to his feet. Indignation and then anger swelled within him as he looked at his friends scattered motionless on the rough pavement.

Amy alone lay face up, the black velvet folds of her dress spread around her like a dark pool in the long shadows of late afternoon. Disheveled light brown hair veiled her eyes. Her face was colorless and her lips parted.

Chad's heart pounded. Starsiders on the wide porch of a two-story red brick building hummed a chorus like the melody of angry bees, gathering energy to cast at him again. Chad was dumbfounded. This was supposed to be the "good" side—the people Amanda had claimed considered the rights and feelings of others. Instead, they had attacked without a word of warning, and for all Chad knew, killed the Star Daughter and her companions.

Barely ten yards away, marble pillars supported the two-story roof above the porch of a building spanning the entire width of the courtyard. This had to be the Starside headquarters. The crowd's rhythmic humming shifted its harmony, warning Chad a second assault was imminent. He smiled inwardly, eager to give it back to them with a bit extra.

He saw the wave's shimmering weight pressing down on them as they added to the churning mass of energy and held it, dammed, above their heads.

With a snap the wave burst forward and tumbled toward Chad and his friends like a tsunami.

With a mental heave, he held the wall of energy in place, his eyes on the Starsiders as he stepped to Amy's side and knelt. Her eyes were closed.

"Ladies and gentlemen," he said, facing the crowd. He wanted to kick himself when his voiced cracked. He cleared his throat and continued, "May I present to you, The Star Daughter."

Chad indicated Amy with his hand, palm up, and walked around to place himself between her body and the gathered people. Mutters broke out from the crowd as he bent over her, placed a hand on her neck and brought his cheek down close to her nose. His heart leapt when he felt the faint beat of her pulse against his fingertips and the brush of her breath as it danced across his cheek. Sighing with relief, he smoothed the chestnut hair from her face.

He checked each of the others before returning to stand over Amy's supine form.

He released the wall of energy he held and allowed it to dissipate harmlessly into the air.

Chad took a deep breath and raised his voice again. "And I am her Champion." Injecting as much confidence and sincerity in his voice as he could, he continued, "If any of you raise so much as a finger against her, I will destroy you."

A collective gasp of dismay mixed with murmurs of indignation. Staff members looked from side to side, or shuffled in place, but no one moved to leave the porch.

"Get someone out here now!" he shouted in frustration. "Take responsibility for your careless attack and get help for my friends!"

Before anyone could respond, shouts erupted inside the building. The large wooden doors groaned open and a group of men and women rushed out. A large, heavy man pushed to the front of the group, his face bright red and sweating. He bellowed, "What is going on here?"

A woman broke away from the rest and hurried to the man. "Your honor, a portal generated in the courtyard."

"That can't be," the man growled, wiping sweat from his forehead with the back of his sleeve. "This courtyard falls within the protective boundaries of the energy screen. No one can cast a portal in or out of this building or its grounds."

Chad looked around, unsurprised to find the portal was no longer there. Too bad, he thought.

"Yes, your honor," the woman continued. "That was why, when the portal appeared, we believed we were under attack. We attempted to incapacitate all who came through. This boy claims to be the Star Daughter's Champion."

"Chad?" A familiar voice called from inside the building, beyond the open double doors. "Let me through."

"Mr. Snider," Chad called, his voice a squeak. He doubted Amy's dad had even heard. Chad coughed and with more strength, shouted, "Amy's hurt. Bring someone to help her."

Mr. Snider broke through the crowd and rushed to his daughter.

"I'm sorry, Mr. Snider," Chad said as he stepped aside, feeling inadequate and small. "I failed you again. They got us just as we came through the portal. I wasn't prepared. I didn't think—"

"Don't worry, Chad." Mr. Snider's voice was thick with emotion. "She's only being held unconscious. We'll bring her around soon. And your other friends as well."

Mr. Snider looked at him from his daughter's side. "They are your friends, aren't they?"

"Yes," Chad said and his eyes fell on Amanda. "Mostly."

Medics and assistants rushed into the courtyard through a gate opposite the pillared building and moved the four unconscious youths onto litters, carrying them back out the way they had come.

"Wait," Chad called to the departing medics.

"It's okay, Chad," Mr. Snider said and put an arm around his shoulder. "We'll follow them. Come on."

As they passed through the gate's high archway and into the bustle of the busy street, Chad pulled himself back into his safe place before he spoke to Mr. Snider.

"I met my father." He said the words quietly so only Mr. Snider could hear.

Chad didn't know why he said it and felt stupid for bringing it up the moment the words left his lips. His face heated with a blush as Mr. Snider angled his head toward him. Chad looked up and saw concern on the man's face.

"We'll need to talk, and soon, but not now. We're going to visit Amy in the hospital, and I've got a place where you can spend the night." Mr. Snider raised his head and looked around before turning back to Chad. "Listen. Be very careful about what you say and to whom. It's almost sundown, so if anyone questions you, just tell them you're tired and you will talk about it tomorrow."

"What about my friends? Two of them were working for the Cloudside. They're good people and I don't want them treated like they're criminals."

"Marie is one of our agents, and she already told us about Felipe."

Chad considered asking about Amanda, but decided it was not the time to discuss her.

31 - Recovery

Chad sat on the edge of a wooden chair across a wide hallway from Amy's hospital room. He leaned on his knees and stared at the floor. A guard at Amy's door had allowed Mr. Snider into the room, but refused Chad access. It seemed like hours ago.

At the sound of approaching footsteps, he looked up and saw the prime minister walking his direction. He knew the man was powerful and commanded respect, but Chad wasn't impressed. Prime Minister Fontaine nodded to him and appeared about to speak.

Chad stood and made sure his mind was completely within the safe place so no thoughts strayed.

"It appears we have some things to discuss, young man," the prime minister said with a smile that didn't reach his beady eyes.

Chad shook his head. "I did what I was supposed to do. Now, I think I should just go home."

"Well." The man drew out the word. "Where is your home? I mean, truly. In the primer world? I don't think so. Not from what I heard of your actions in the courtyard."

"My mother is in the prime dimension. And I really want to be back with her, back in school where everything is normal."

"But you're not normal." The prime minister stepped closer, his bulk trapping Chad against the wall behind him. "You have power and potential and you need to be here to develop those things properly."

Though the man spoke calmly, he took a handkerchief from his pocket and wiped at his forehead.

Chad squeezed to one side and stepped back, out of the man's reach. "I'm really tired. It's been a long day. Can I talk to Mr. Snider? I think he knows a place where I can stay."

"I've made arrangements for you," the prime minister said and reached out to take him by the arm.

Chad felt small bursts of energy probe the borders of his protective shield and it made him angry. He had to fight the urge to gather those bits and shove them up the prime minister's nose.

"No," Chad said and raised his voice well above what was appropriate in a hospital. He didn't care. "I really think I should talk with Mr. Snider first."

The man's smile faded to a frown as he glared at Chad just as Mr. Snider stepped out from Amy's room.

"Ah, your honor," Mr. Snider said with a forced smile. "You've come to check on the patients?"

"Yes," the prime minister harrumphed. "Of course. And to have a talk with our hero."

"Mr. Snider," Chad said before the prime minister could continue. "I really need to speak with Amy, but that guy at the door won't let me in, or even check if it's okay."

"I'm sorry," Amy's father said. "I wasn't thinking. Go on in while I have a chat with the prime minister."

Mr. Snider nodded to the guard who waved Chad into the room.

Amy sat in the hospital bed, its back raised nearly upright. A sheet covered her legs and waist and her hands were folded neatly in her lap. Her hair shimmered in the faint glow of the bed's overhead night light. Chad paused. She looked like a queen. Across the room Marie and Amanda carried on a quiet but animated conversation from their beds. They giggled as Chad stepped toward Amy. He scowled, thinking they were laughing at him. When they appeared oblivious to his presence, he continued to the chair and sat next to Amy.

"Hi, Chad," Amy said. "I really want to thank you for coming to get me. I think things would have gotten pretty bad if you hadn't shown up."

"Well," Chad mumbled. He really didn't want the other two listening in on this conversation. "I had to. Since it was my fault you got dragged off by Derrick."

"No," she said and held her hand out toward him. "It was my fault. I grew up knowing who I am and what would be expected of me. I should have been more conscious of what was going on."

She dropped her hand to the bed and, looking down, shook her head. Chad had never seen her sad before and the sight of her quivering lip startled him. Amy was always cheerful and positive. Seeing her this way nearly made Chad sick. Her hand nearest him was balled into a fist as if she were trying to squeeze the life out of the sheet in her grasp. Chad placed his hand lightly on hers and she relaxed.

"I'm sorry," Amy said and looked at him, her eyes brimming with tears. "I should have recognized Derrick. I should have warned you about him." She heaved a deep sigh. "I should have warned you about me."

"No," Chad shook his head. "I think it had to be this way.

He stood up to give his fidgeting legs something to do. "I'm your Champion. I needed to figure that out on my own. To learn what it means, and to prepare for what's coming. I think if you had told me what was going to happen, I would have run away and hidden, and messed the whole thing up."

Chad realized with chagrin he still held her hand as she squeezed his and smiled, blinking away the remnants of her tears. He turned and saw Marie and Amanda staring at them, wide-eyed and smiling. Embarrassed, he dropped Amy's hand, sat back down, and leaned in to whisper so the others wouldn't hear.

"I need to tell you something," he said haltingly, and looked at her face, trying to judge her emotions. She appeared attentive and mildly concerned.

"Okay. So," he murmured, searching for a good starting place. Finding none he just pushed forward. "When I couldn't find you anywhere at the school, I went to your house and talked to your dad. He didn't seem surprised you had been taken away and said that since I gave you to Derrick, I would have to be the one to go into the dimensions and get you back."

"Alright," Amy said, carefully. "That makes sense."

That it seemed so reasonable to Amy unbalanced him even more, but he pressed on regardless. "Your dad said I could only give you away because I had an emotional connection to you. That I was in love with you."

Amy was smiling now. "Don't worry, Chad. It can't hurt you."

"What?" Chad asked, surprised she had interrupted him. "Oh. No. I know it won't but—"

She looked at him expectantly.

He scowled. "Just let me finish before you make fun of me, okay?" he asked and she nodded contritely.

Chad started over. "I'm your Champion and I don't think we're all done yet. Or you're not, at least. But I don't think I can be your Champion anymore."

He stopped again, expecting her to interrupt him, but she only frowned and looked at him expectantly.

"When I think of champions I picture the Knights of the Roundtable. And knights have to be, well, dependable, honorable, or maybe, I mean, faithful. And I'm not. I want to be, but I don't think I can." Chad finally managed to clamp his mouth shut on his rambling.

"Chad," Amy finally interjected. "What are you trying to say?"

He ducked down closer to her as he looked back at Amanda and Marie to see if they were still listening. He whispered, "I haven't been faithful to you. I think I'm really in love with Amanda. When I'm around her, I completely lose my head. I tried to kiss her one time. And another time, in the dimensional chamber, I did kiss her."

He blushed bright red as he heard Amy laugh and say much too loudly, "Chad, you don't have to be in love with me to be my Champion."

From their sudden silence Chad guessed the other two girls were now staring in his direction, but he refused to check. He whispered low and hoarse, "But your dad said... Well, I thought I was... but, I couldn't help myself."

He stopped jabbering and scrubbed his hands across his face, scowling over his shoulder again at Amanda and Marie who were both grinning from ear to ear.

He finally asked, "How am I supposed to help you if I can't control myself?"

"Chad," Amy said, humor lingering in her voice. "You don't have to worry about that. Amanda told me all about it."

"She *told* you about it?" he demanded and stood.

"Yeah," Amy said. "And there's something you need to know about her, besides her being almost five years older than either of us. You've probably seen, as your own control of the power has developed, that it gets easier with practice."

"Right," Chad agreed. "It comes easier to me now. Almost without my having to think about it."

"Right," Amy said. "That's the way Amanda is. When she was younger, she learned a little tune that attracted boys to her. She liked all the attention they gave her, so she used it almost constantly. After a while, she didn't even need the tune anymore. Unfortunately, she often forgets she's doing it, and inexperienced or unsuspecting boys fall victim to it all the time."

"Would this unconscious skill of hers sound anything like a tinkling bell melody?" Chad asked.

Amy nodded and laughed. "You should see her bedroom. She has more flowers than a florist."

Chad shook his head and sat back down. "Sometimes I hate this place. I never know if what's happening to me is real or not. I don't know who to trust, or if I can even trust myself."

The two girls behind him were silent, but Amy spoke, "I'm sorry. I know it must be disorienting..."

Chad snorted a laugh. Trying to hide his embarrassment, he wiped sweat from his forehead. "Disoriented doesn't really come close to how out of place I feel in this world.

"Amy, I'm sorry, I got you into this mess. If I hadn't been such a spineless wimp, I could have stood up to Derrick, and not sold you to the Cloudside." He looked at his hands. "You should find another Champion. I don't think I can take any more of this."

"Boys are hardheaded and egotistical, aren't they?" Amy said to him, though a twinkle remained in her eyes.

"What's that supposed to mean?"

It means... Well, consider this. When did you agree to give me up in exchange for that game player?" Amy sat up straighter in bed.

"When Derrick told me..." Chad started to say, but stopped.

"Did you say, 'Sure thing, Derrick. She's all yours. Let me go get her?'"

"Well, no, but—"

"No. You never gave me to him. Derrick used you to get to me. He got lucky. He didn't know you had a connection to me or the ability to manipulate energy. Without those two things in place he couldn't have tricked you out of the Champion's position, leaving a void he could step into. In fact, he never figured out that he had assumed the Champion's role. He just thought he was extra clever and tricked me into following him."

Disgusted with himself for his own cowardice, Chad stood and headed for the door.

"Wait, Chad," Amy demanded quietly.

When he turned back to her, she spoke more sternly. "You *are still* my Champion and you still have an important role to perform. You need to be on your game, now more than ever. Go get some sleep and something to eat. If I know anything about Prime Minister Fontaine, he has something in mind for both of us and it won't be for our personal benefit."

An inkling of resolve welled up from deep inside and he nodded slightly.

"Okay. I'll see you in the morning."

#

Chad was surprised to find the hallway empty.

He knew where Felipe's room was and strode to the closed door. He tapped lightly before turning the knob and stepping inside. The bed was empty and Chad jumped when Felipe spoke from a chair to his right.

"Hello. May I help you with something?" the older boy asked.

"Oh. Hi," Chad said when he saw Felipe sitting, fully clothed, with his legs stretched out and crossed at the ankles. "You look like you're feeling okay."

"Just a little tired," Felipe said. "I'll be happy to leave here as soon as I can."

Chad agreed with him. During their short conversation Chad thanked him for his help in their escape and for caring for Amy. Felipe stood and clasped Chad's hand and placed his other hand on Chad's shoulder as they walked to the door.

"Be true," Felipe said as he released his grip.

As he made his way back to the hospital lobby, Chad wondered if that was a standard good-bye on Felipe's world, or if he was giving Chad some special council.

Mr. Snider stood at the glass front doors, his back toward Chad, and peered out into the night.

"Amy seems to be doing alright," Chad said as he reached Amy's father.

He turned a weary smile on Chad and said, "She's nothing if not resilient."

Chad tried to look through the darkened window where Mr. Snider had been staring but only saw his own tired face. "You said you had a place for me to stay. Do you think they have something I can eat? I'm really hungry." Chad's stomach growled right on cue.

"Oh. Of course." Mr. Snider turned to Chad. Lines of worry creased his brow. "I'm sorry. I'll take you there and you can get something to eat."

Chad tried to keep his voice casual as he asked, "Did the prime minister leave?"

"Yes. He left," Mr. Snider said, concentrating his attention on the glass doors again. Sounding equally distant, he added, "We'd better go, so I can get back."

"What's wrong? Are my friends safe?"

"Yes. They'll be fine. There will be guards posted around the hospital and the girls' room. Felipe's as well."

To Chad's ears, Amy's father was trying too hard to sound unconcerned when he continued, "It's more to keep people out, than to keep anyone from leaving. And I'll be back here as soon as we get you settled."

The night air was warm and reassuring as they walked along the sidewalk. The occasional pedestrian smiled in greeting, and Chad saw the Starside phase-shift on all of the people they passed.

They walked in silence for a few minutes until Chad asked, "Will we be able to go home now? And, you know, go back to normal?"

"We'll get you home in the next day or so. Amy too," Mr. Snider said, but from his tone Chad could tell he had more to say. Chad waited for the man to continue.

"I don't think Amy will be there for long," Mr. Snider finally said. "By tomorrow afternoon, everyone on both sides will know who she is, and there will be no hiding her in the prime dimension or here, either. It will be safest for her in the compound. When the time comes, we'll gather our things and relocate the whole family back to this dimension."

They stopped outside a red brick house. Light shone through multiple paned windows. Mr. Snider nodded toward it. "This is the home of my closest friend. We've known each another since we were children, and I trust him with my life. You can spend the night here. Before we go in, you need to understand something else."

Chad's heart dropped again. With everything that had happened lately he was getting used to having it beat from the pit of his stomach, rather than in his chest where it belonged.

Mr. Snider's voice was only loud enough for Chad to hear as he said, "Amy's task has yet to be completed. She still needs you here to help and protect her."

"That's all fine to say," Chad grumbled and turned away. "But I don't think I can do this. I didn't grow up here. I'm just not made for this."

Mr. Snider put his hand on Chad's shoulder. "If what our HQ defense unit says is accurate, then you are an extremely powerful young man and you need to be here where we can teach you how to use your talents and protect you."

"I don't need your protection," Chad snapped, and immediately felt guilty. This man had always been kind to him, and because of Chad's actions, had spent the last few days worrying whether his daughter was dead or alive.

"You're probably right," Mr. Snider agreed evenly. "Still, this is the best place for you. Don't worry about it right now. Get something to eat. Have a shower and sleep. I'll be by early tomorrow morning to get you back to the hospital.

Chad nodded, but said nothing as he followed Mr. Snider up the matching brick steps to knock on the door.

32 - Ultimatum

The cool air of early morning felt good against the heat of Chad's face. His eyes burned and his head felt thick from being woken so early. Hulking trees appeared as mammoth shadows arching over the gas street lamps. Chad struggled to match Mr. Snider's long strides as they hurried down the dark lane.

"We're not going to the hospital," Chad said. "Where are we going?"

"The prime minister had all four of them moved earlier this morning." Mr. Snider bit off the words. He clicked his tongue. "I'd stepped away to get something to drink and when I came back, they were gone."

"Sounds like they were just waiting for you to leave," Chad said. "How can they take Amy without your permission?"

Mr. Snider nodded. "I'm sure the prime minister came up with some semi-plausible excuse."

They rounded a corner onto a wide, divided street with large trees and flowering shrubs on the center island. More gas lamps followed the sidewalk on both sides of the street. A few hundred yards farther along, they outlined a circular roundabout before the tall, wrought iron gated entrance to the prime minister's mansion.

As they reached the closed gates, a guard stepped from a small building and approached and spoke to Mr. Snider through the bars. "May I help you?"

"I'm Ted Snider," Amy's father said. "I was told my daughter has been brought here. I wish to speak with her."

"One moment," the guard said. "At this time of the morning, I must check with my supervisor. I'm sure you understand."

"Of course." Mr. Snider frowned, folded his arms and stepped back from the gate.

They stood at the curb of the roundabout and looked back down the street.

"Why do they use gas lamps?" Chad asked randomly. "Wouldn't electric be safer and easier?"

"Probably," Mr. Snider said. "We can develop a dimension any way we want, any time period or era.

The catch is, once we have begun, it's difficult to create something from a different era. It can be done, of course—the hospital is technically advanced—but it takes much more energy and effort."

He looked up at the lamp and said, "And there is just something about this romantic period in history; the people seem to create and gather to this type."

The metallic clank of the gate's lock told them the guard had returned.

"You may enter," the guard said. "But the boy will have to wait in a separate room, and will not have access to the others."

The hairs on the back of Chad's neck rose and a hot flush of anger burned across his face, but he said nothing. Arguing would do him no good. He couldn't help anyone if he was locked outside the grounds. Grinding his teeth, he stepped inside his mental safe spot and held his tongue.

Inside the mansion three men approached Chad and Mr. Snider. The first stepped forward and said, "Mr. Snider, I am Harold des Blaines. I will take you to your daughter. These two gentlemen will keep the young man company."

The two hulking men stepped forward to bar Chad's way. Each was more than twice his size.

Chad suddenly learned the limitation of his skill in the control of energy. He had no special strength against normal human muscle power. He pictured himself drawing up energy, swirling it about and bowling the two ogres over. Unfortunately, there was no energy lying about to gather up, amplify, and wield.

The guards walked Chad into a side room.

"I thought you were supposed to be the good guys," Chad sneered, but couldn't get a rise out of either of the men.

"Whatever," he said, and sat in one of the blood-red leather chairs along the far wall. Eyes closed, he forced his body to relax.

He reached out with the innate energy of his mind, as he had done outside Thrush's house, to read the energy and thoughts of the two guards. He approached them carefully to avoid alerting them to his presence, but no matter how he probed, their mental shields remained intact.

He expanded the probe out past the small room to search for another mind to touch. Yet as he searched, the early hour caught up with him and he drifted off to sleep.

For the second time that morning, Mr. Snider shook Chad awake.

"Let's go," Amy's father said. "Prime Minister Fontaine wants to talk with you."

Chad was still struggling to shake the cobwebs from his mind as he stepped into the prime minister's office. Felipe and Marie stood to one side, concern etching lines of worry across their faces. Amanda sat on a cushioned couch, her face expressionless and pale.

Chad and Mr. Snider joined Amy who stood before Fontaine's desk.

"Mr. Baker," the prime minister said without preamble. "I do apologize for the confusion this morning. I must beg your cooperation in this matter."

He looked at Chad as if waiting for a reply. Chad didn't know what he expected—he wasn't about to agree to anything. Especially an arrangement the prime minister was trying to manipulate him into accepting without question.

When the silence had stretched well past uncomfortable levels, Chad finally said, "Well, it depends on what you want me to cooperate with. So far, I've been playing this entire adventure by ear. I wish someone would just speak plainly to me."

"Okay," Fontaine said, "Plainly put, we are letting you go home."

"*Letting* me?" Chad asked, perturbed at the prime minister's wording. Only a few hours before, going home was the only thing he wanted. Now that he was being given *permission*, anger ignited within him. Then it hit him. The prime minister's voice had the same ring of deception to it that Amanda's had at times. Chad snuck a glance at her on the couch and wondered if she was somehow related to the conniving politician.

"Yes, letting you," the prime minister repeated. "If we wanted to keep you here, or perhaps eliminate you, it would be a fairly simple matter. But, instead, we are acquiescing to your request and will extend a portal to the prime dimension in the general area of your home. We only ask that you promise not to return. If you do, you will be eliminated."

"I'm confused," Chad said. "I haven't had much sleep recently and maybe it's making me hear things wrong. Did you just threaten to kill me?"

The prime Minister's eyes were dark, narrow slits that shot razors at Chad, though he said nothing.

"Huh." Chad grunted at the man's silence. "And what about Amy, does she get to go home, too?"

"This is her home," the prime minister stated flatly. "She has work to do here and will be a great asset to the aims of the Starside.

Chad reached out to Amy's mind, reading her feelings and trying to see if her wishes were the same as Fontaine's. Her thoughts were dark, confused, and discouraged. Then she was suddenly gone. Her mind closed off as if she, or someone else, realized he was trying to reach her mentally. With a start Amy turned to Chad, her eyes wide with surprise—a physical confirmation of the confusion he had encountered within her.

"You don't have to stay, Amy," Chad said. "With Amanda and Marie, we can open a portal into my backyard. We can go right now, if you want."

Amy looked back to Fontaine.

The prime minister laughed. "Sending a portal to the prime dimension isn't as simple as you believe, Mr. Baker. Besides, as you can see, she knows her duty. She will be a great boon to our struggle for control, or rather," he seemed to scramble for a moment after his little slip, "for the spread of freedom and prosperity throughout the dimensions. With the Star Daughter by my side all will want to join in our cause."

"You're no better than Caltone." Chad nearly spat the words. "All you want is control and power, not to help people."

More than anything, Chad wanted to go home, to be with and help his mother—to live a normal life. But something in the Starside leader's attitude affected him. Like a pinch or the poke of a needle, the feeling started low on his back and climbed his spine. His own commitment grew and resolved when he spied the look of determination on Amy's face as she turned back to Chad.

"You said if I return, I will be eliminated," Chad said as he stepped to stand closer to Amy. "Fine. Then I'm not leaving. Amy is the Star Daughter and I am her Champion. I have to be here, to protect her, and to assist her."

Protect her.

Fontaine was clearly a threat to Amy, the Star Daughter. As her Champion, Chad was obligated and empowered to protect her from anyone and everyone who stood as a threat to her, including the prime minister. To his surprise, a new melody resounded, originating from the safe place in his mind. Where he had no defense against the two thugs previously assigned to guard him, now, energy infused Chad from within.

With a whoosh, pearlescent bubbles of energy flashed up around him. Immediately, he threw a protective shield around his companions and Mr. Snider.

Guards burst through the door. As they entered, Chad threw a wall of energy at them, encasing each guard in a shimmering mass of power, preventing them from moving, and eventually barricaded the doorway.

Chad dropped the protective shell from around Amy and together, they approached the prime minister's desk.

"Prime Minister Fontaine," Chad said. "As Amy's Champion, I will do everything in my power to protect her. No matter who or where the threat originates from. If Amy remains here, I will remain with her."

"Caltone was on the verge of using me to subject our society to his will," Amy said, her voice strong and clear. "I won't allow you to do the same. The Starside's goal is true freedom for all people, Prime Minister, not subjugation masquerading as such." Then she turned to Chad and whispered. "The two of us, working together, have the potential to make it happen."

She nodded to him.

Chad leaned closer to Amy's ear. "You're the one with the real power. Can't you just tell them to stop acting like jerks and let us go? As a diplomat, they would have to do exactly as you command them."

"That does look like the simplest solution. However, a diplomat's power has far reaching repercussions— consequences I'm not ready to face just yet."

Chad frowned. "Right. So, what should I do?"

"Let them go."

Chad turned his back on Fontaine and faced the immobilized guards at the back of the room. With a dismissive wave, he dropped the protective barrier around Mr. Snider and his friends. Then, after a prolonged glare at the guards in their shimmering, golden prisons, he nodded his head. The bubbles of energy disappeared like water soaking into the sand. Chad stood with his arms folded across his chest, feet planted, and mentally dared any of the guards to move.

"Prime Minister," Amy continued, "I will aid neither you nor Caltone nor anyone else in turning a single person's will against their true allegiance. Whether you threaten us, incarcerate us, or set us free, the result will be the same."

She turned and, head held high, motioned for their party to follow. Together, the little group strode out the door.

No one tried to stop them.

Epilogue

Chad climbed the few wooden steps to the stage in his junior high school's auditorium and accepted the scholarship check Mr. Satoro had promised him. Grinning, he looked out across the assembly of seventh and eighth grade students. Some of the kids laughed, others mouthed threats. But Chad didn't care. He mentally muted the roar of their combined thoughts and searched out his mother's mind where she stood by the door in the back. Mr. and Mrs. Snider stood beside her and all waved, snapping pictures.

As the assembly ended, the choir sang and though there were dozens of students, Amy's clear and pure voice was the only one Chad heard.

The End.

The Page of Love.

Thanks for reading *The Price of Friendship.* I hope you enjoyed it. There are two more books in this series that I have written and am in the process of editing for publication.

If you'd like advance notice of how those books are progressing, go join my newsletter at www.norvaljoe.com. You'll be directed to the sign up page.

For joining the newsletter, you'll get a free short story about a character from my other series, "Shooting Stars", in which Chad and Amy make the occasional cameo appearance. The story is about Doug, a vampire, and about how he came to be the antagonist of that series.

Thanks again,

Philip